PRINCESS NAI

AND OTHER STORIES

PRINCESS NAI

AND OTHER STORIES

JAMAL SAEED

Translated by Catherine Cobham

Published by ECW Press
665 Gerrard Street East
Toronto, Ontario, Canada M4M 1Y2
416-694-3348 / info@ecwpress.com

Editor for the Press: Michael Holmes / a misFit Book
Copy editor: Kenna Barnes
Cover design: Jessica Albert
Front cover artwork by Asmaa Ali El Amin

LIBRARY AND ARCHIVES CANADA CATALOGUING IN PUBLICATION

Title: Princess Nai and other stories / Jamal Saeed ; translated by Catherine Cobham.

Names: Saeed, Jamal, 1959- author | Cobham, Catherine, translator

Description: Some stories partially written in Arabic but not published. All stories first published in English.

Identifiers: Canadiana (print) 20250214865 | Canadiana (ebook) 20250214873

ISBN 9781770418042 (softcover)
ISBN 9781778524882 (ePub)
ISBN 9781778524899 (PDF)

Subjects: LCGFT: Short stories.

Classification: LCC PS8637.A355 P75 2025 | DDC C813/.6—dc23

This book is funded in part by the Government of Canada. *Ce livre est financé en partie par le gouvernement du Canada.* We acknowledge the support of the Canada Council for the Arts. *Nous remercions le Conseil des arts du Canada de son soutien.* We would like to acknowledge the funding support of the Ontario Arts Council (OAC) and the Government of Ontario for their support. We also acknowledge the support of the Government of Ontario through the Ontario Book Publishing Tax Credit, and through Ontario Creates.

Canada Council for the Arts
Conseil des arts du Canada

ONTARIO ARTS COUNCIL
CONSEIL DES ARTS DE L'ONTARIO
an Ontario government agency
un organisme du gouvernement de l'Ontario

PRINTED AND BOUND IN CANADA

PRINTING: FRIESENS 5 4 3 2 1

Purchase the print edition and receive the ebook free.
For details, go to ecwpress.com/ebook.

*

To Catherine Cobham and my other three sisters:
Asmahan, Khadijah and Roza Saeed

Contents

Princess Nai, The Flute Princess

My grandfather used to laugh — a lot.

"Grandpa, Grandpa," I said, running up to him in front of our house. "I just saw a goldfimsh!"

"What's a goldfimsh?" he asked.

"The bird I see when I walk along the farm path with my mother."

"You mean a goldfinch!" Grandfather said. He laughed and gave me a hug. He always laughed when I said things like that.

*

I soon lost the ability to talk about the goldfinch in this innocent way. I finished high school and came to Damascus like many other villagers.

A few months later, as I was returning to my apartment in Damascus after dark, I followed my usual routine: put my key in the lock, turned it and switched on the light. Then I saw six men I had never seen before, positioned all around the room and pointing guns at me — five Kalashnikovs and one pistol.

"Who are you? How did you get in here?" I asked. I wondered for a split second if they were thieves before realizing the truth. Seeing handcuffs on their belts, I knew these were Mukhābarāt, the government's secret police, and since they had scattered my books and clothes all over the floor, I presumed they must have found the pamphlets hidden in my mattress, the ones that condemned the killing of a political prisoner under torture.

"Shut up!" shouted the man holding the pistol. "Get your hands up and face the wall!"

As I turned I noticed that the soft thing I had stepped on was a sky-blue shirt. It was the last gift I received from Laila before leaving my village, and before she broke up with me. As I raised my hands over my head, the thought came to me that Laila, always fastidious, would be angry with me for stepping on this fine piece of cloth. When one of the men pushed me against the wall, I moved my foot off the shirt. Surely Laila would forgive me if she knew that I'd been forced by the police to tread on her gift.

Other men grabbed my arms, twisted them behind my back and put handcuffs on me. My head was at an angle, one cheek forced against the cracked plaster. From this awkward position I could see the pamphlets I had hidden were now on the table. They were to have been distributed that night.

I imagined I was wearing Laila's sky-blue shirt and that a gun went off. I pictured my blood flowing, the red staining the blue of the last present I would ever receive. I looked down at the floor where I would fall among my scattered things. That's when I saw her lying on the floor, broken and crushed, the holes in her body bent into arcs. The princess. The sight roused me from my fantasies. I was incredibly sad. A boot had smashed her mouth and torn the lips that had so often touched mine. I could feel the heel of the boot as if it were against my own lips.

As the six men pulled me out of my apartment, I looked back for one last view of the princess lying discarded among the rest of my life's detritus. I never set foot in that place again.

*

One autumn evening far in the past, so long ago that it seems as if it happened in another lifetime or to another person, I was walking behind my mother on a narrow country path through our neighbor's farm. I shouted, "Mum, look at that bird! Such a sweet bird. The color on its wings is like the sun."

"It's just a goldfinch," my mother answered. She was not impressed. But knowing the name of the bird was not enough for me. Why didn't Mum say anything about his beautiful feathers? And couldn't she see the astonishment on my face or understand the love I felt for the tiny creature?

The bird perched on a hawthorn tree at the side of the field, right by the edge of a river and some woods. I ran towards the bird, expecting my admiration and amazement to be reciprocated, but he flew away before I could reach him.

"Why doesn't the bird trust my love, Mum? Why did he fly away?"

"Stop your silly chatter!" my mother ordered. "I have a lot on my mind."

But it wasn't silly chatter to me. I watched as the goldfinch flew into a clump of reeds at the edge of the river. It alighted on the top of the tallest reed and its weight made the delicate plant bow its head, while the rest of the reeds waved their tasseled hats in welcome. I smiled and took a step forward, and that's when I felt someone grip my bony shoulder. Next came a sharp smack on my bottom.

"Don't go near the reeds," my mother hissed in my ear. "They're full of snakes. A snake bite could kill you!"

Later when I saw my grandfather, I told him about the goldfinch and how he landed on the head of the princess of the reeds.

"The goldfinch chose the princess. He chose the princess, right?" I asked.

My grandfather laughed. "Yes, of course. She is the princess of all the reeds for sure."

*

The next day I found myself standing near the clump of reeds again. Their waving green tassels formed a carpet of green, undulating like waves on the ocean. I heard my mother's words again: *Don't go near the reeds. They're full of snakes. A snake bite could kill you . . . kill you!* But the obsession with finding my reed princess was pounding through my veins, and this clump of reeds was where the sweet bird had landed. He had to still be there. And the fact that the place was forbidden made it irresistible, full of secrets I had to know.

So, on that faraway autumn afternoon, defying my mother's warnings, I walked through the reeds. I had to meet the princess, as well as profess my love to the goldfinch. But he had ignored me. When I found him, well, I would ignore him too. But I didn't have the chance. The goldfinch wasn't there among the reeds.

"Where are you?" I shouted. "I want to ignore you."

Maybe he was flying above me, and so, up to my knees in water, I searched the sky. A flock of sparrows fluttered there, but they seemed insignificant and worthless. I was looking for that beauty of gold and black and red.

After a while I gave up on finding the bird. In truth I became desperate. But the princess was still there, somewhere in the crowd. The green carpet of reeds looked more beautiful from a distance, but from inside it was clear the clump was made up of single plants, each one the same as the other. I had only one aim: to discover which reed was the princess. This was my mission, but it was not easy to distinguish the princess from the other reeds. I tried to pick up signs that might help in my quest. I watched how the leaves moved and listened carefully to the sound of them rustling; I heard the birds talking in their own language, and at some point all the voices transformed into a single voice inside me, which convinced me that the reed at my right hand was the princess. I felt happy to have recognized her and decided to take her away with me.

"Now I know who you are," I told the princess, taking hold of her slim body. I reached into my pocket and pulled out a knife I had taken from my mother's kitchen that morning. The sparrows flew away, and I pushed back the princess's attendants with my elbows and cut through her stem. I nicked my hand with the knife, causing it to bleed a little. My blood dried on the princess's body. I left the forest happy, dragging the long reed behind me, riding it like a green-tailed horse, stirring up dust as I walked.

At home my mother hit me because she had been searching for her knife all morning. She hit me again because I had cut my hand. And a third time for disobeying her and going into the reeds.

"Why are you hitting him?" demanded my grandfather, who was smoking in the corner of our house. My mother tried to explain, but he dismissed her with a flick of his wrist. She left the house angrier than ever.

"So?" Grandfather asked, and I told him I had brought the princess of the reeds home with me, explaining how sparrows and other reeds had pointed her out to me.

"You understand their languages?" he inquired, his eyes wide. I nodded enthusiastically. Grandfather laughed harder than ever.

"But where did the goldfinch go?" I asked.

"Don't worry, he'll be back," he said, eyeing the long reed.

"When?"

"Patience! In a little while. You'll see. In the meantime, when the reed dries and becomes stiff . . . I mean when the princess dries . . . I'll make a shabbabeh, a reed pipe, and you'll play wonderful music on it."

A little later grandfather took the reed princess away from me as I was using her as my horse outside in the dust. He took her to our mud-brick house and hung her upside down.

"We must let her dry straight," he said.

*

Some weeks later I watched as grandfather took the reed off the wall and began stripping away her dried leaves and withered tassel crown. He fetched wood and started a fire and then thrust two metal skewers into the heart of the flame. As they became red hot, Grandfather contemplated the length of the princess's slim body, now dried and stiff. He chose a section that had just the right roundness and thickness.

"I think I can get two from her," he said to the air, and he took his whittling knife and cut out a large section from the middle of the reed. Then he cut it into two sections, one shorter than the other. He took the shorter one and blew into its hollow shaft. It made a flat, dead sound.

"That'll do."

And then he took his knife and quickly carved a rounded notch at one end.

"This is where you will blow," he said.

Next he placed his fingers along the shaft and marked the spots with his knife, five on the front and one on the back. He took one of the two skewers out of the fire. It glowed hot, and I held the cool end with a rag. Grandfather burned holes into the shaft where he had marked the spots and placed the iron back into the fire. He was done.

"Here you go, Grandson, your shabbabeh," he said, and handed me a flute like the ones other boys in the village played. I put my fingers on the holes and blew into the reed, and a shrill squeal tore through the air.

"I'll show you how to play it later. But now I will make a Nai, a bigger flute." He picked up the longer section of the reed princess.

Now the look on Grandfather's face changed. He seemed to be saying a strange silent prayer while he stared at the princess's body, moving it tenderly around in his hands, touching it with one finger here and another there, again marking her with a nick of his knife. These cuts seemed to be farther apart than on the first flute. As he worked his hand quivered and twitched while his eyes seemed to peer into the princess's soul. And all the while as he touched her, she lay in his hands obedient and quiet. He took the other skewer from the fire, and I noticed how the tip was now pulsating with an even redder and hotter glow.

Hiss cried the princess, as the first hole burned through her reed body, causing smoke to rise into the air. I watched how the red of the poker danced in my grandfather's eyes as he worked.

Hiss, hiss, hiss, she sighed, as more holes were burned into her. Grandfather then took his carving knife and made the curved notch, her mouth, through which she would receive the breath of life. He was almost finished.

It was the end of the day and time for my grandfather's glass of wine. He poured some of his wine into the princess's mouth and then drank the rest himself. His hands were visibly trembling now. I was overcome by an inexplicable feeling of reverence. And then my mother's father raised the princess to his lips and softly blew into her mouth. She sang her first note, and as my grandfather's gnarled fingers danced over the holes on her body she began to sing. The sound was mesmerizing. I felt myself floating on a wave, like the sea of green tassels above the reeds.

Suddenly I was brought down to earth by a dark anger. I looked at the long slender body of Princess Nai in my grandfather's hands and the short child's flute in mine.

"You've made Princess Nai for yourself and left me this child!" I shouted, throwing the shabbabeh to the ground. "I want the princess!" I shouted even louder. "She's mine! You've cheated me, Grandfather!"

My grandfather looked at me in astonishment. And then, just like that, he held Princess Nai out to me. I took her and looked down at her then up into my grandfather's eyes. I felt confused. He laughed.

"Okay, then, she's yours," he said. "Play."

I held the princess, but my fingers were not able to reach all her holes no matter how much I tried to stretch them.

"The holes are too far apart," I complained.

"They'll be fine as you get older," he said, laughing again.

"When will that be?"

"Soon. Don't be in a hurry."

*

The "soon" my grandfather talked about came to pass. I grew up. My fingers could cover the holes of the flute, but I still couldn't make my princess sing like my grandfather. But every time he offered to show me, the dark anger returned. And so my progress with the princess was slow. But I continued to try and, when I did, Princess Nai protested in pain. That's when my mother would cover her ears and threaten to smash the princess over my head. I still didn't know how to let my soul whisper in the princess's mouth and make her sing sweetly.

*

It wasn't long after that when Laila began to avoid looking into my eyes.

"I think . . . we . . . I mean to say . . . I believe . . . it would be better . . . if we broke up."

"What? Why?" I was trembling, too shocked to voice the question in my heart: *All I can think about is my love for you. How can you think about breaking up?*

At the time I did not understand Laila was a separate being from me. She owned her body and soul, so she had the right to use them as she wished. Laila left me, and I panicked like an animal that knew it was about to be slaughtered. The world seemed incomprehensible. I ran into the house and grabbed the princess from the drawer where I kept her and rushed into the street, heading for the oak woods on the edge of the town. There was the same river running through the forest where I first found the princess, and I stood on its bank, my soul in pain. I joined the river's babbling cry and shouted into the air, "Laila, Laila, lama sabachthani? Why hast thou forsaken me?" There was no answer except for the sound of the rolling river.

I sat on a rock and put Princess Nai's mouth close to mine. I blew into her and finally a song poured from her that captured the pain of an innocent teenager. I closed my eyes and heard how the beautiful lyrical sound spread through the whole of the forest. It was so pure I could feel many gods sitting down around me to listen. As I continued to play, I saw them in my mind. Some watched my fingers tremble over the princess while others enjoyed wine from skins brought from the distant heavens. Still others floated languidly in the river, their eyes closed as they lived the emotions I was sending out into the air. The eldest and wisest of the gods came over to me and put a hand on my shoulder. I felt his tears fall on my face.

"What a gentle heart you have, my son. Pain is harder when it's borne alone."

As I continued to play, I saw the rocks, oaks, rivers and reeds disappear. All that was left was the wise one's face, his long, sacred beard wet with his compassionate tears. I began to cry. My sobs filled the air where the music had been. When I opened my eyes and wiped the tears away, I looked for the gods, but they were invisible to me and to everybody else. They had come streaming out of Princess Nai to find their way into the air and lived only in my memory.

Not long after the princess had trained me to deal with her, she raised her mouth to mine one summer evening and began to sing. I saw my mother approach and was about to stop, but the look in her eyes told me she was no longer going to threaten to smash the princess over my head. And so Princess Nai and I began to sing for my mother, about an evening when we walked together, about a sweet goldfinch and a hawthorn tree near a country river. About the boy I was and the man I was becoming. Although she didn't understand the words hidden in the music, they spoke of things my mother knew, like a familiar secret. When I lowered the princess from my mouth, my mother looked at me with an expression I hadn't seen for a long time.

"Play more," she said, "your music touches me." And she placed a hand on her heart.

*

I did not become a famous musician.

No journalist interviewed me, so I could tell them I did not like to play from notes on paper. The lines on these pages were like prison bars to me. Nor did I tell anyone that the flute is much purer than all the stringed instruments, because the flute lets you pour your soul into her directly, while stringed instruments need an intermediary — fingertips, a bow or a pick. Because of this, to my mind, something of the soul is lost.

As I gained in ability, all that anybody needed to say was "Play for us," and the melody that was in Princess Nai flowed out, free and uninhibited. And I continued to refuse to write the princess's melodies as musical notations. All those in the village for whom the stories were meant would be able to hear them, and when I rented my room in Damascus, her songs floated out of its cracked window and imposed themselves on the air of the city.

It was in that room that I put up a small shelf and lined it with a length of turquoise silk.

"This is your bed," I whispered to my princess. After that, no matter whether night or day, if a new melody was forming in my mind, I'd feel the princess there too. Then I'd wake up and we'd join together to sing.

*

A long time ago I was taken from that room, and the princess was left shattered on the floor. She was grabbed from her bed and brutally destroyed. For a long time, during my years in prison and after I was released, I often wondered about my princess's fate. I couldn't bear to accept that the owners of the house had swept her up and thrown her in the trash, to be taken away the next morning by a garbage truck. But that is probably the truth and the reason why, over the years, I have thought about how many beautiful roses end up in the stomachs of those vehicles.

I can no longer walk with my mother to the river because she's too feeble to make it that far. And when I see a bird now, to me it's just a bird, as my mother would say. I have lost the great mind I had as a child. And although I have gone back many times to the clump of reeds, I have lost my way of seeing that things may not be what they seem. Anyway, my grandfather is no longer alive to carve a reed flute. If he were, I would ask him, "How can I meet a princess again?"

I think my grandfather, who always laughed a lot, would laugh at this too.

Tadmur prison, 1985. Edited, 2022.

The Scent of Pine Trees

This story was published in a magazine in Beirut in 1982 after being smuggled out of al-Qal'a prison in Damascus.

I no longer remember when I first heard the word *holy*. I may have used it in an essay when I was at school without knowing what it meant. I did write about things without knowing exactly what I was talking about. For example I once wrote, *Memory is a bell that chimes in the world of oblivion*. I didn't understand the meaning of the phrase, but I liked it when I read it on the back of a picture and used it in an essay about spring, which made my elementary school teacher, who was very thin, laugh out loud.

Let's return to my story about *holy*.

It was a warm day. Its warmth still lives in my heart, and I recall it in these cold pale yellow days. It rises spontaneously to the surface in times of crisis and when I'm dreaming. The pines were green as always and Hana was a lively young filly and I was a lad from the mountains. We entered the forest and the scent of pines. Virgin land like a headstrong girl not yet used to kissing, and so the forest forced us to go the way it chose, and we were like conquerors.

That was all beautiful. We reached a narrow track, one of the tame parts of the forest, and then we felt tired, maybe because the path ahead of us was suddenly smooth.

Hana lay down impulsively under a huge tree where the ground was covered with pine needles.

"Are you tired?" she asked me.

"No," I replied, like all teenage boys from the mountains when asked such a question. I sat down panting, and she knew I had lied.

The sun was hidden behind the dense green needles that covered the branches of the huge pine tree, and her eyes were shining, and at the edge of the narrow path some beautiful, bright daisies caught my eye.

"Are you thirsty?" I asked her. She raised her head and looked at me, nodding.

"Yes, I am, but I—"

"I know a spring nearby," I interrupted.

I jumped up, and she followed me to a small pool, and we saw how the sky and the pine needles were reflected in the heart of its slow-moving, calm surface and felt compelled to kneel until our lips touched the water.

We returned to the shade of the great tree. The sun sank farther in the west. We brushed the dry pine needles off the ground like children playing a game. The shade became more invigorating. We both lay down, resting our heads on our hands. She began twisting a tiny twig in her fingers, putting it in her mouth from time to time. She took hold of my hand that lay at my side. Looking into my face, she said, "Your eyes are beautiful." I was happy she said that, and happy my eyes were beautiful, but I remained silent. I didn't know how to respond and couldn't think of anything to say. I think she realized that, or knew I was embarrassed. She lay down again.

"What are you thinking about?" she asked gently.

"Nothing."

She smiled with unforgettable sweetness. In my mind's eye her smile is as sweet today as it was then. Behind that smile I could read, "I know exactly what's going on in your head, you stupid teenager. What else does a man think about when he's lying beside a woman and they're alone together?"

Calmly and confidently, she said, "If a person's awake, he must be thinking about something."

I looked at her like a child trying to avoid a math question. I was a child and the world in my child-head and child-heart was a playground. She knew how confused I was. Despite that, I felt like a tiger reigning over the vast forest and a hawk spreading its wings across the sky. Hana was the icon the world obeyed, so she transformed it into my playground and me into a child and a tiger and a hawk, then set me free to roam.

I was drinking life in, or that's how it seems to me now, taking deep drafts of the forest, the sky and the shining eyes of the tigress lying beside me. Her eyes were fierce, gentle and pleading all at the same time. I was silent, not fully understanding what was going on inside me. All I knew was that I was happy, strong and relaxed.

She undid the top button of her jacket, and the edge of her bra became visible, along with the channel between her breasts and the part where they met her chest. The roundness of her breasts moved my world. I wanted to become a kiss and dissolve on top of them. Her eyes sparkled and the world was spinning and swaying and my heartbeats were visible above the light in my eyes.

"The world is beautiful," I said, embarrassed.

She knew the world at the time just meant the roundness of her breasts and the edge of her bra, where the pines, the sky, the earth and my heart dissolved. The familiar light and the friendly sky suddenly seemed astonishing, and the earth and my heart much more beautiful than any of the people I knew. Her cleavage appeared mysterious, great, magical, and the lace stretched taut on her chest more splendid than an artist's creation, more than just material for sure. She smiled. Her face took on a different color, softly calling out to me. Her smile and her eyes indicated an interaction that was about to happen and would surely light up the universe. The scent of her filled the air, mixed with the delicate scent of the pine trees. As it entered my nose, I felt it mingling with my blood and it's still there. Everything was suggesting that we should begin to light up the world, this world that we inhabited and that inhabited us. That's the way I think in situations like this, but I was too stupid to know where to begin.

She broke through my fear and cowardice and stupidity, putting her arm gently round my neck. Her hand was trembling like her voice, and the whole world seemed to be trembling as she said, "You stupid man. I love you."

Then I was trembling too. I needed all my strength to say timidly, "Me too. I love you too."

I'm embarrassed when I remember how my voice shook. It seems ridiculous now.

We sank into a beautiful world. I kissed her repeatedly. My heart was on my lips, and I offered it to her in every kiss. That beautiful lace encountered a voracious hand that tore at it violently. Now it's the hand of a prisoner relying on the past to escape the stupidity of prison. I buried my head in her breasts and felt I was covering them with God and goodness. Our clothes became a small chaotic bed, with some scattered around us, and the scent of the green pine needles was our cover. The sky was the roof of our house and love a master, a great god blessing us and whispering in the air close by: "Blessed are the two of you, blessed are all the lovers on Earth, for they are its masters."

I lay down beside her. We were panting, exhaling warmth. I looked at her face; her eyes were half closed. All the tenderness of the world was concentrated inside me, and I gathered it up into a kiss that I deposited onto one of her half-closed eyes. Her faint smile was like the scent of the pine trees.

I never again looked for the meaning of the word *holy* in a dictionary.

al-Qal'a prison, 1982.

Sunstruck

I imagine a man in his forties who stood on his doorstep one morning and spat into the air, believing he was spitting in the face of the world. Addressing life he said, "I will live you, however much you bark and bite, you bitch. I will live you and so will all my sons."

And I imagine a young man who wrote to his father in a faraway village: *Damned money again! This city is a money sink, Dad.*

The same evening he wrote on the back of his lecture notes: *This city isn't just a money sink. It's a sink for everything, for people most of all.*

In the city described by the young man lives a young girl. For those who celebrate the occasion, there have been 13 celebrations of New Year's Eve since her birth. She has only participated in the creation of a snow sculpture 3 times and memorized more than 20 songs that she sings when she's alone.

The young girl woke up slightly late that morning, rubbed her eyes, yawned and sprang catlike out of bed. She washed her face, sprinkled water on her hair and dried it with a faded pistachio-green towel. She arranged her hair, then messed it up and arranged it again. She repeated the process many times, saying each time, "It's better like this." She went back to the first style and stood on tiptoe, craning her neck.

"If only I were a little taller." She raised her arms above her head and was pleased to see the fuzz under her armpits and notice how her breasts had begun to stick out under her dress. She took hold of the dress and pulled it tight over them.

"They'll grow," she said, smiling to herself.

The young girl sat on the edge of her bed.

"My father has gone to work. Why does he never laugh? He's old and doesn't like to laugh. My brothers are playing ball now. If they destroy the flowers in our fat neighbor's garden or smash any of the windows, my father will beat my brother Iyad. Please, God, keep the ball away from that fat cow's flower beds. Why did she plant her roses where they play? My mother's gone to the market. She buys zucchini for us every day. I don't like that dish . . ." The girl stood up and went to sit on the chair by the window.

The window looked out onto a street, passersby and a few cars. Above the street is a sun, and beside it green trees and boys playing and laughing. Through the window drifts a beautiful female voice: "The children are playing sweet games . . . playing and not getting bored . . . playing . . ."

The young girl stood up. She was embarrassed when they said to her, "You're a big girl now," but she didn't like them treating her like a little girl. She sat down on the chair again.

"The world is so dark," she muttered and sighed. "We should color it white, write on it in white chalk. But when winter comes and the rain falls, the white chalk will dissolve and the dark world will still be there. The world will be like our black cat Rana. I made a white costume for Rana, but my mother tore it off her and Rana was black again, even blacker than before."

The young girl had named the cat Rana after one of her classmates and whenever she thought about the cat or called "Rana, come here!" she smiled to herself and remembered her classmate.

But she didn't smile to herself that morning, or remember her classmate, even though she remembered the cat. She put her finger in her mouth and bit it hard.

"The world is black as night," she said. "The black will go away if a fire breaks out."

Then she thought sadly, *But fire kills. Why don't we light up the world without using fire?*

Her question made her happy and she thought of it as her own discovery! She went towards the front door where there was a stove that her father always described as a genuine Primus stove. Beside it lay a box of Horse matches, and along with the picture of the horse on the front of the box, there was a black fingerprint and smudges of oil. The girl lit a match, and when it burned down and hurt her thumb, she flung it away in fright and sucked the wounded finger.

"The world is still dark," she said. "Matches go out, candles go out, but the sun never goes out."

Again, the girl was delighted at her discovery. She dug out some of her school notebooks and began drawing suns on them, then drew suns on the wall above the mirror. When she went to school next day, she drew suns on her classmates' notebooks, on the blackboard and on the classroom benches.

She always instructed her suns to light up the world because it was still dark. Next she learned to draw suns in the air and gave them instructions too. Then she began to scoop up suns in her cupped hands and throw them out of the window into the street. She scattered a handful of the beautiful suns over her mother's hair and her mother's reaction mystified her.

"What's wrong with you, girl? What are you doing?"

She thought for a while before she gave Miss a green sun drawn on lined paper. She distributed suns all over her schoolmates' heads.

Why are they laughing like that? she wondered sadly.

Her family began to feel scared. Everyone was saying their daughter was crazy, obsessed with suns. Their fear grew when they saw boys chasing her, crying, "Give us suns!" and she scooped up a handful of air and threw it at them, saying, "Here. Tell them to light up the world. Don't forget."

The boys pretended to catch the suns and put them in their schoolbags laughing. Her family was dismayed by this crazy obsession with suns.

What I didn't imagine, what was all too real, was that I was in cell number 4, which the prison guard sometimes called "Chalet 4." In fact he sometimes called me "Chalet 4," and he did mean me, not the small cold room. For example, he used to yell, "You've got two seconds to do everything, Chalet 4!" Then he'd open the door. He meant I had to go to the lavatory, wash my face and come back in and get breakfast. This was "everything," and I had to do it, rather than the building, which never moved from its place. It was clear he meant me, and I always took more than two seconds.

What I didn't imagine, either, was that I was constantly looking at the faint light that came into the cell through a small opening from the bulb in the corridor, along with shouting and angry voices cursing and cries of pain — a mixture of many sounds, the sound of the key in the door of the cell holding its own terror; there are some things that aren't worth mentioning when writing this story.

I had plenty of time to try to extract the jagged bits of cement from the floor — I failed. I had plenty of time to train myself to see in the poor light and to stare at every detail of cell 4. On the wall I saw a sun drawn erratically, an irregular circle with lines around it. My fingers passed over these lines and traced the circle often. Many things emerged from that circle, most of which I've forgotten.

With a coin I had on me that they'd missed when they searched me, I tried to write something underneath the sun on the wall, the sun that looked so much like a little child, but I didn't know what to write.

I was sorry when they transferred me to cell 9 because I hadn't written anything below the sun of cell 4.

I still don't know how the girl obsessed with suns got into cell number 4.

Perhaps she threw one of her suns in the air and it landed in the cell and drew itself on the wall.

al-Qal'a prison, 1982.

That Night

The wind that night was like Mayada.

Mayada — for anyone who wants to know more about her — is the one who forced this comparison on me. Mayada's femininity dominates the things that are happening near her. Or if you wish, things cease to be present, and nobody notices them when Mayada is standing there.

Mayada's femininity can inhabit any part of her body and exercise its power, so glaringly evident that it's impossible for me to remain composed and behave like a respectable male. She exercises her femininity and her beauty in the way she moves, the sudden turn of her head as she flicks back a lock of hair, in her smile, in her calm demeanor. What puzzles me is whether Mayada does this spontaneously, and her spontaneity becomes part of that unsettling beauty of hers, or whether she does it deliberately, knowing that she is beautiful, and consequently the movements of her body become an extension of the femininity that confuses both men and women.

I love talking about Mayada, but Mayada is not the story here. (I think readers would understand this digression if they knew Mayada.)

The wind that night was not really like Mayada. It was cold, icy and dark, and made a whistling sound, while Mayada was not at all cold or dark, and didn't whine or whistle. The power of that wind and the sound it made are very different from the power of beautiful Mayada, who drives people crazy and makes hearts flutter, lost and weary, like the bird flying around that night.

The bird suffering that night was an ordinary little sparrow, the sort we see in front of our houses, on the trees in our villages, on the roofs of our cities, everywhere we go.

That night he was flying to outrun the wind. He would find it in front of him, and if he retreated, he would find it behind him. A wind overflowing with wind, just as Mayada overflows with Mayada. Wind in all directions. Wind wherever he flies. Wind laden with snow, scattering snow everywhere, making his wings wet with snow. Bone-piercing cold on all sides, and darkness, and the darkness hides the whistling of the wind. The wind whistles constantly, and the little bird flies. However far he flies, there is cold, dark wind and snow.

He was saying disconsolately, "You're all against me," and flying onwards, searching for someone different from those whom he addressed as "all of you."

A snowflake that had dropped off his wings said, "I didn't think the Earth was so small. I never knew it would tremble and shake me off its back. Now I'm destined to remain floating in endless space." Then it murmured something about a crazy wind and how it would prefer the company of wolves. But that night it gave its body to the wind that engulfed all the whispering and murmuring, and wove trumpet sounds from the cold, indifferent whistling.

All of you know the sparrow for sure. You watched him last spring choosing a prominent spot, a telegraph wire to be precise, so he could jump his wife as often as he wanted, not caring what you thought, even if you thought it shameful and stared harder so you could see more. Then he would fly off warily, haphazardly, from his narrow marriage bed. But all this has nothing to do with that night when the wind blew fiercely. That night the solitary bird, beleaguered by the wind, took refuge in the small window of an old house. Once through the window, he found himself in a tiny, cramped sky that was still more spacious than a sky overflowing with wind and darkness, and was suffused with warmth and light.

The old house didn't care what the wind was doing, and its stern silence didn't betray any of its dreams or concerns. Its face was that of a professional gambler who never gives anything away. The old house had lived for many years like the professional gambler's pocket, sometimes full, sometimes empty. Even that night, when a lot of things happened around it, it remained where it was, silently waiting. (That's what houses are like. They remain where they are, silently waiting, and nobody knows what they are waiting for, deep in their long silence.)

Before the bird entered, two old people were lying by the stove, a man and a woman, their eyes closed, sometimes hearing what the wind was saying and sometimes indifferent to the thousands of souls lamenting and quarrelling at the heart of the storm. They knew more than this wind but understood nothing of the commotion made by those uneasy souls. They were listening instead to the warm whispering of the fire, and it didn't occur to them that the wind was crazy, constantly trying to say in a thousand tongues: "I'm like Mayada, I dominate everything around me." But it couldn't possibly be like Mayada.

(It seems important I escape from Mayada in order to be able to talk about that night. Notice, for example, that I have the urge to digress again to say sarcastically to myself: *Can Mayada really spoil your story about that night? Is your story so important? Abandon your story, you idiot, and focus on Mayada.* Mayada is not the problem; it's writing or speaking or anything that distracts you from her. In my mind I accept with a smile the jailer's crudely sarcastic remarks as he flogs me. But regardless of his opinion, I shall apologize and carry on with my story about that night. Or no need to apologize, for digressing is what I do, especially when it comes to Mayada . . . But my digression has lasted too long.)

When the bird entered the house, the sound of its wings woke the two old people from their reverie. (Wings, as you all know, speak rapid, troubled, incomprehensible words whose letters run into one another and are almost indistinguishable from one another).

The two old people were calmly mulling over images of people, places and events, chewing on their simple history that was devoid of conquests, glorious exploits or great, complicated adventures. They were closing their eyes on their history, such as it was, and when the bird came in through the little window, they opened their eyes together, raised themselves up on their elbows together, looked at the bird together, and together it became clear to them they were not dead yet.

They weren't waiting for death, nor were they expecting to win any battles in their lives. They were waiting for Khalid's return. Khalid was their youngest son who was imprisoned one night, a different night from the one I am writing about here. They didn't know why he was imprisoned, and after they learned from his older brothers that he had been reading certain pamphlets that — that *what*, they didn't understand — they tried unsuccessfully to see him, unable to believe he would stay away for so long. Khalid was engaged to Mayada, and Mayada broke off the engagement two years after he disappeared, as she said, "Who knows? He may never come back. And nobody knows how long he'll be in prison for."

His old mother heard what Mayada said, and the meaning of her words was much clearer than the wind that night and far harsher. Although Mayada appears strong, she told me she couldn't look the old woman in the eyes, and she just wished she would let her help her — as she had done before — with the laundry, the cooking and the sweeping.

That night Mayada told me she wanted to die. I laughed to hide an overwhelming sadness and told her she was still thinking like a teenager. She looked reproachfully at me and left the room in tears, believing I was just one of the large group of people who didn't understand her. When I looked up at the ceiling, I saw Khalid's face saying quietly, "Be kind to her." For a moment I thought nobody understood me, either, not even the ghosts that emerged from my head and took up residence above my bed. Then when I thought a bit harder, I took pleasure in saying, without much conviction, "Nobody understands anybody."

This time I truly apologize for my digression. What's important here is those two old people. After the little bird had roused them from their daydreams and recurring visions, it flew around the narrow space for a while. Then, tiring of that, alighted on the edge of an old bed in a corner of the house, whose white sheets had turned brown even though nobody had slept on it since the cat was killed by a gunshot. A fighter who couldn't find anyone to shoot shot the cat, who was sleeping on the bed in the corner.

The bird looked all around him, cautious behavior inherited from his ancestors, which was better than inheriting nothing, like the robin, whose innocence led him constantly into traps. Despite the bird's wariness, the old woman was able to approach him nimbly, after she and her husband had observed him in silence as he perched on the edge of the bed and shook his feathers and then went quiet.

The man was watching his wife. Both of them forgot everything and looked at the bird. The wind was no longer audible, and the whispering of the fire had ceased. The bird had obliterated all the sounds and erased the people, places and events that had filled the heads of the two old people a little while before. Now the woman stood below the bird, and the man began to watch the approaching battle. He was moved by the sight of her as she tried to maneuver herself into a suitable position and prepared to catch hold of the bird, and then by the delicate way she extended her hand to him. Who was going to win? Would she catch the bird, or would he fly away? Her performance was exciting in itself, regardless of the outcome, and the man found himself watching wide-eyed.

The old woman managed to catch the little sparrow as skillfully as a cat. The man laughed but lacked sufficient enthusiasm to clap and cheer like football fans when their team scores. He hid his enthusiasm and remarked spitefully, "Well done, you're as graceful as a teenage girl and just as stupid."

"Don't be afraid. Calm down," she said, stroking the back of the frightened bird, who hadn't escaped the storm just to become a hostage in a hand that prevented even his wings from expressing their fear. Then she looked at her husband and said, "Do you think I'm old like you?"

The man made a rude gesture and said, "We'll see about that tonight."

The woman smiled. "That's all you're good at," she said, then sat down and stroked the bird, asking him why he'd gone out on a day like this, sensing through her fingertips the scared beating of his little heart and reassuring him. "Don't be afraid, son."

"It's true, it's a male!" proclaimed the man, observing the bird's round, clear eyes and anxious head movements, and the woman agreed, noticing the dark patch on the bird's neck. The bird's soft feathers were irresistible. "Give the little scoundrel to me," he said, and the woman held the bird out to him.

"Be careful," she warned. She let the bird go before the man had taken a firm hold of him, and the bird circled the room at speed once more. The woman stood up and watched him flying angrily around.

"Calm down you crazy bird," she entreated, but the bird didn't respond and flew furiously out through the little window, at which point she could hear the sound of the storm loud and clear. She looked towards the window.

"Come back, son," she called. "Nobody goes out on a night like this."

"Do you think he can understand you?" laughed the husband.

"Didn't I tell you to be careful?" she demanded angrily.

"You let him go too soon," said the husband.

"You're always the same," she said angrily. "You can't do anything at the right time."

They began arguing, and the wife would have dug up a whole long history had he not brought her back to the runaway bird, saying sarcastically, "Are you afraid he'll catch a cold?" At this she burst into tears.

The man tried to placate her and said with a conciliatory smile, "Have you gone crazy? A bird landed in our room, then flew off! So what?" But she went on crying.

"What's happened to him?" she said tearfully. "The cold will have eaten into his bones. Tadmur's a cold place, and they don't give them any heating."

The man did his best to reassure her, as he always did when she mentioned Khalid.

"I know a lot about prisons. They have heaters, blankets, beds and clothes in prison. Somebody told me. A man who was in prison ages ago . . . in the days of the French. He knows everything. And he said to me, 'Don't worry about Khalid. Don't worry about him. He's a tiger.'"

He repeated this and other things until she stopped crying. He managed to get her to spread the bedding out beside the stove, and when he lay down beside her he tried not to let her see that he, too, had a heart and eyes that shed tears and nobody to lie to him or reassure him.

That night the two old people fell asleep later than usual. They lay there in silence, and when they closed their eyes, they saw Khalid trembling and crying for help. The wind continued to whistle over the old house and blow gusts of snow all around it, proceeding on its way, indifferent to the black darkness of that night. The darkness was taciturn, silent, indifferent to the wind, while the bird, confused, said, "They're all against me."

Mayada's window was in darkness. She had turned off the light and gone to sleep. Sleep was happy in Mayada's embrace, bathing in her warm blood cells. The old house looked on in silence at the cold, the darkness, the wind, the snow and the bird.

"They don't understand anything," it said and then carried on embracing the two old people it had known for a long, long time.

The wind that night was like Mayada. But not exactly.

Tadmur prison, 1986.

The Climbing Rose

The children flocked around the rose tree whose death had been expected for more than four hours after Abu Fahd dug it up.

When they reached the tree, it showed no signs of death at all; its flowers and petals were still smiling their fresh smile, confidently exhaling the same scent as before they were uprooted, and its leaves had not yet offered any response to the death that had begun in the morning.

Suddenly the tree had become accessible. Before, when they wanted to pick its roses to give to their teachers so they'd smile and say, "Well done," the children were forbidden to go near it. They ran up to the tree and began eagerly picking the roses, since they'd given their teachers flowers of every other kind.

They couldn't believe at first that Umm Fahd saw them and just watched them in silence and did nothing.

Ramez Malul, the boy with untidy hair, got tired of picking the flowers and announced that the rose tree had been dug up because a large snake slept among its branches at night and licked the flowers, poisoning them. Some of the children believed him at once and threw their bouquets down on the ground, rubbing their hands in the earth and spitting as if they had swallowed poison. Amer said the children who stopped picking the flowers were "donkeees." (That's how he pronounced the plural of *donkey*.) They were donkeys according to him because they didn't know that the poison evaporated in the morning when the sun rose. Then he smelt the flowers enthusiastically.

"Ha!" he exclaimed. "They smell nice. Poison doesn't smell like that. It smells horrible."

Haitham looked at Amer, then wiped his snot on his shirt-sleeve and addressed the children who'd started to pick the roses again.

"You're all going to die," he told them. "Come along, Rana. Let them die. Come with me." But Rana, busy gathering roses, stuck out her tongue at him and carried on with what she was doing.

Haitham moved away with Ramez and his group. They went over to a muddy patch of ground to make mud pies.

"Is it true the snake sleeps in the rose tree?" Haitham asked.

"Yes, it's true," answered Ramez confidently. "Tomorrow they'll give the roses to the teachers. The teachers will die, and the school will close down."

Haitham was glad the school was going to close down, but Rana mustn't die because she had bitten Usama for him. Usama was the blond boy who picked on Haitham and provoked him so he could make fun of him. For some reason, it seemed to Haitham that the dying rose tree was turning into a big snake biting Rana's hand. He stopped rolling the clay into a ball.

"How can the snake sleep on thorns?" he asked Ramez. "Roses are nothing but thorns."

"Snakes don't care about thorns."

"Will Rana die?"

"They'll all die."

Haitham wiped away his snot with his shirtsleeve again, threw the lump of clay he was holding at Ramez and ran off. Ramez ran after him, shouting, "I'll shit on you, you bastard!"

The other boys abandoned their unfinished mud pies and the tree and the children, who were still picking roses, and chased after Haitham and Ramez.

*

Umm Fahd continued to look at the children and the tree lying there on the ground like a bride slaughtered on her wedding day. She saw how the children laughed and shouted together, competing to see who had the biggest bunches of roses and who could pick fastest.

Imad and Fahd were like that when they were young, she thought. She stared at the garment in her hand, turned it over and gave it another rub with a gloomy expression quite unlike her usual expression when doing the laundry. She raised her head from the washbowl that lay meekly in front of her and stared into space as if she could both see and not see the children and the tree and time that tears things apart.

When Umm Fahd had finished washing her own clothes and her husband's and her daughter Nadia's, the rose tree was no more than a heap of branches with a few green leaves here and there, and some spots of blood from the tender fingers pricked by the thorns. Umm Fahd did not see these details. The death of the tree had become more obvious now the children had left, along with their shouting and quarrelling and laughter and the roses distributed around people's houses. Umm Fahd's house had grown quiet, its windows looking out at the tree's scattered limbs, maintaining their silence and composure, concealing their secrets and sorrow.

*

Fahd's moustache was already visible on his upper lip when he came home one evening long ago, holding a sapling that resembled a small smooth green stick.

The same evening he planted the rose.

"This type of rose climbs like a grapevine," he told his sister Nadia, "but the flowers aren't like the rose we know, they're smaller."

They bet on whether the rose would climb over a trellis like a grapevine and agreed to wait four or five years to see.

"They've grown up," remarked Abu Fahd to his wife, as they listened to Fahd and Nadia talking.

Umm Fahd wept because her son Imad had died before he could grow up with them.

*

Fahd never got to say to Nadia, "Can't you see how it climbs like a grapevine?" nor remind her of their old bets, because after planting that small green stick he disappeared for 48 days. They put him in the belly of a car designed for removing him and he disappeared. Umm Fahd saw them shoving him into that car, and ten days later when she was rolling vine leaves to make yabraq, she remarked, "If it was the Mukhābarāt who came and took Fahd away, then it was human beings like us, but these weren't like us."

She was surprised that the women who had gathered to help make yabrak didn't understand what it meant to be like us but not like us, and she carried on trying to explain: "If it wasn't the Mukhābarāt who took Fahd, then God alone knows who it could be making people disappear."

*

While Fahd was away, the rose tree climbed until it formed a wall on the west side of the garden, a wall that changed color with the changing seasons. The tree became familiar like everything else there: the smell of the pantry, the color of the wall, the hill visible from the south window. But Fahd went away before it became familiar. He never saw its beautiful, familiar green, nor the way it made wonder and familiarity coexist like brothers. He did not see it when it blazed with the white of its roses, tinged with a blush of faint embarrassment because it knew it was the most beautiful tree in the garden and everyone was looking at it. Fahd did not see how, when it grew old, its yellow-grey hair made it dignified and venerable.

*

By the remains of the rose tree Umm Fahd wept, perhaps because she remembered Fahd. When they took him away, she couldn't do a thing. They took him just like that, as if he had no mother or father to defend him. That day Abu Fahd realized how powerless he was, and he burned all the books that he thought caused those who read them to disappear for indefinite periods of time. He wanted to do something, but neither Umm Fahd nor Nadia responded to him when he tried to provoke them to react. They did everything he asked but said nothing, and when he burned the books, they just cried.

By the remains of the rose tree, Umm Fahd wept, perhaps because she couldn't say to Fahd, "Look. That's your rose tree. It's grown. I protected it and didn't let anyone pick a single bloom from it." She repeated this sentence many times as she looked at the rose tree in its moments of brilliance, when it seemed as if it would tear itself free of its roots and fly. Perhaps she wept because she loved that tree and now she was losing it, just as she had lost Imad forever. Perhaps she wept because, without the rose tree, the house looked like a woman whose head had been shaved so her scalp was exposed. When Umm Fahd heard the Mukhābarāt had shaved Ghada's head, she began to shake all over. She knew Ghada was one of Fahd's closest friends. Maybe she wept for all these reasons, or for other reasons. She never told anyone why but just kept looking at the scattered remains of the tree.

On one occasion she said reproachfully, "Didn't I water you every day? Did you really have to let your roots spread into the sewage pipes?" Then she carried on weeping silently and said nothing more, as she didn't want anyone to hear her talking to herself out loud, didn't want other people to smile pityingly and say, "Umm Fahd's gone crazy. She talks to herself."

Tadmur prison, 1985.

A Lonely Young Man on a Rocky Shore

He remembered his grandmother's pockmarked face as he walked slowly over the crumbling rocks on the beach.

(She would have liked to spread her heart out like a warm tender beach for people to walk on.)

He remembered the day his uncle returned with his family from living abroad. His grandmother went up to his young cousin to hug and kiss him. The little boy took fright and ran away from her, staring with terrified eyes at her pockmarked face and taking refuge in his mother's skirts, shrieking. Everyone was embarrassed by the child's behavior, and his grandmother touched the smallpox scars on her face, her fingers moving quietly, exuding sorrow. Trying to put an end to the confusion that filled the room, she looked at the little boy and declared so they could all hear, "You're right, little one. I'm scared of my face too." Then she added softly, "Smallpox is an everlasting curse. Even when I'm dead, you'll only remember my pockmarked face."

(My grandmother's eyes were windows. Every time I looked into them I could hear her soul weeping.)

He felt a little awkward as he walked over the rocks, as if he was trampling on the pockmarked face of a huge grandmother. He remembered science textbooks: erosion, lime, decay, mineral salts. No, the rocks were much more like his grandmother's face than the textbook description of them. He was interrupted by a sea breeze, passing gently up his shirtsleeve.

(This breeze is as soft and delicate as Ghada.)

Suddenly a long question confronted him with the expression of a stern schoolteacher.

"You're walking over the rocks on the beach, not on your grandmother's face. Stop these stupid hyperboles, calling a passing breeze 'Ghada' and the softness of Ghada and I don't know what else. You know Ghada has snot in her nose just like anyone else. Would you marry Ghada if she had smallpox?"

The young man stood before the question like a confused schoolboy, remembering some heartfelt phrases he had once jotted down in an exercise book: *Ghada is light in a pitch-black world, fresh dew that revives the soul when it's surrounded by desert, a horizon in a world that has lost its horizons. The soul dances around her eyes like a butterfly, and only around her eyes can butterflies sing their sweet songs.*

The question started to make fun of the young man.

"I didn't ask you to talk about Ghada. Would you marry Ghada if she had smallpox? It's a simple question, smart-ass."

Impulsively, the young man protested. This "smart-ass" annoyed him a lot.

"Love is one thing, and marriage is another," he began enthusiastically. "Love is a warm light the soul pours over the world. Melodies flow through your blood, and the stones dance in time to them. A beautiful madness takes you wandering through the vast spaces of your soul. Marriage, on the other hand, is a tradition that nobody has ever consulted me about."

The question made fun of the confused young man's answer and began spinning a web tightly around him, skillful as a spider.

"Philosophize about love and marriage as much as you like. Do you love Ghada?"

"Yes," replied the young man eagerly.

"Do you want somebody else to marry her?"

"No. We have to live together. I mean, I wish we could."

"And if she gets smallpox?"

The young man shook his head vehemently and ran away from the question. He looked at the sea. A bird folded its wings and swooped down onto the surface of a wave, while another spread its wings and rose up off the same wave.

"The whore says no. The poor wretch runs after her, his blood on fire," the question said.

A wave broke on the rock beside him, and spray landed on his face.

"The sea is spitting on the question, that gets out of my head, asking, 'How can she be a whore if she says no? And anyway, who says she's female?' The sea is right. And the seagulls could be two males or two females, each wanting to catch a fish whose curiosity and boredom led it to discover the meaning of a seagull's beak, even if this knowledge was rapidly obliterated by death. Why do we sometimes enjoy swearing?"

He remembered an old friend. In his last letter to him he'd written, *I didn't know I'd miss you and your filthy tongue so much.*

(Where is he now? He used to look for an occasion to swear, as if he was competing with somebody to invent bigger and better insults.)

They used to share a small room in a big, crowded city. The young man said to his friend, "Isn't this room of ours a cozy world?"

Infuriated, the friend began to curse: "Bastard, how can you call this disgusting hole a cozy world? Aren't you ashamed? We're in a city that mocks us every second. All we have here is time farting at us and cars rushing by. Now the city just has to shit on our heads to make the 'world' even cozier."

"You're always so foul-mouthed. You do nothing but grumble and complain. Life goes on and doesn't listen to you."

"Naturally, because it's too busy listening to your crappy compliments."

"Isn't there anything in it for us to love?"

The friend looked sad.

"Even the things we love are taken away from us," he said, "and we can't do anything to hold onto them." Suppressing his sadness, he went on, "Ghada will leave you twice, once because of the smell of onions from your armpits, and again because if you persist with the onions, you'll be unable to fulfill your duties as a man. True, you may think an onion looks like a testicle, but my biological intuition tells me that onions cause idleness and even impotence if one eats nothing else. If you vary your diet, you'll be able to see that Ghada isn't the only thing that makes life beautiful. Learn, dear fool, to see life clearly, not to adorn it with your fantasies, for, like you, it's the child of a thousand whores, however much you dress it up."

"First, I can't be the child of a thousand whores all at once."

"And secondly?"

"Secondly, you're confusing life with these bad times that aren't worth living, and yet we put up with them."

"And thirdly? But please no bullshit."

"Thirdly . . . listen. I'll be serious. Although I look exactly like my father, I don't care if I'm the son of the man they say is my father or someone else's son. A man and a woman got together, and I came into this world. That's the important thing."

"What an earth-shattering discovery! So you didn't just drop from the clouds. I'm going to tell people that I was living in the same room as a great scientist, a shitty room on the outskirts of the city."

"Listen, man, don't interrupt me. Sometimes I wonder whether the moment I came into being was a moment of blazing passion between a man and a woman, or if it happened when they were performing boring marital duties, I mean, sometimes boring."

"Nobody, not even your mother, can answer such a stupid question. No offence. But I've just had a flash of inspiration. Listen. I came into this world involuntarily, suddenly found myself confronted by a complex mixture of comedy and tragedy. As you're stupid, I'll make things simple: This life is a coin. The ruler's signature is a farce, and the inscription on the other side of the coin is a tragedy. But I can leave this complex mix whenever I wish."

"Are you thinking of suicide, genius?"

"Didn't I tell you that you wouldn't understand? I said I could leave this world whenever I wanted to. I didn't say I was going to do it. I could hit my head against the wall every morning but I don't."

"So all this talk is just to say nothing, idiot."

"I didn't know I was talking to a wall disguised as a man. Listen, I'm going to squeeze life to the last drop, live it even if it turns into bare rocks."

The young man looked at the sea, imagining it as an expanse of decaying rocks.

(Yes, he'd be able to live among these rocks. If I saw him, I would ask him if he'd marry his beloved Huda if she had smallpox.)

The question stretched contentedly.

"And what about you? Would you marry Ghada if she had smallpox?"

(Where are you, my friend, when I need you to choose a suitable insult for my woeful head?)

His friend said to him once, "There must be a woman in this world whom I can love more than any other woman and who loves me too. But it's stupid for a person to spend his life searching for this woman. Every time he meets a woman, he'll think she's not the one, until a woman turns up who banishes all his misgivings and doesn't let him question whether she's the one or not. Nobody can go all around the world getting to know every woman who exists. Life's too short. I loved Huda," he added. "She became the one. I no longer wanted to look for another woman. Huda was all women in one. I'll be sad if I find out one day that she was a bitch!"

(He and Huda were the stuff of love songs. Is it possible that I'll find out one day that Ghada wasn't worth all the time I spent thinking about her? Are there diseases fouler than smallpox that infect the soul? Would you marry Ghada if she had smallpox of the

soul? Woeful head, spare me your moaning. I love Ghada because I love Ghada.)

He looked at the sea and saw a steamship approaching.

(Steamships are cows without heads or legs. They're born like that. What do they have in their stomachs?)

He could see his friend smiling his usual smile and saying, "These cows have teeth in their bellies that chew up sailors' lives."

The lonely young man, who walked beside the sea as darkness fell, smiled at the memory of his friend's face. One day the friend made a cutting from a newspaper. On it was written, *Sagittarius: If you manage things well, you will be safe for the rest of the month.* He stuck the cutting on a plastic box that we used to call "the treasury" and said, "It's no coincidence that we both have the same star sign. I bet you everyone who lives a dog's life is a Sagittarius. Does this journalist, the idiot whose advice we're going to act on, think we dine in fancy restaurants and spend our evenings drinking champagne with girls in nightclubs? It would be better if a frog jumped into his mouth and paralyzed his hand so he couldn't write."

Then he began giving instructions on good management, assuming the expression of a clown, then of a treasury secretary, then an army commander and finally a preacher delivering the Friday sermon. He rounded it all off with a string of curses which led me to say, "Here we are, both of us in the care of Sagittarius, so why do you insist on making your tongue a cesspit?"

"These are dirty times. This city drowns us in its filth, so how are we supposed to keep ourselves clean? Are you angry because I said we are like dogs? There are a lot of dogs living lives we can only dream of."

The young man smiled as he remembered his friend's conversations and how he used to curse. He felt the urge to fly and immerse himself in the recent past, which seemed so sweet despite everything.

The steamship grew bigger. *(Steamships carry people from shore to shore — he laughed — I'm such a genius. They also carry bales of cotton, Ronson lighters, car tires. Car tires roll along the road and then spend their old age in those cold places where bodies are stuffed into tires — he didn't want to remember those places. Ships also carry arms — arms for war, not for sport. Addressing the sea, he said, "Why do you get involved with weapons? War is a death factory.")*

He was a child again, hating war and wondering, as children do, *Why are they fighting?* He remembered the old headline "War against War." He also remembered that Hiroshima wasn't destroyed by the plague or disfigured by smallpox, but by the bomb. He'd laughed bitterly back then as he read the headline out loud.

"What a witty journalist," he said, and his friends laughed with him. Their hearts trembled when they saw Hiroshima still suffering her death and coming into the room to reproach them: "Do you think it's funny?" They hid their embarrassment in silence.

He remembered many headlines and old school songs. Various notions began crowding into his head, in different colors, red, white, grey:

"Homeland: is the Earth really a homeland for humanity?"

"Freedom, Justice, War."

"War and militarism are evils that should be wiped off the face of the Earth."

He quickly banished war and the military from his mind, not wanting their company on his evening walk, but the headline "Hiroshima wasn't destroyed by the plague or disfigured by smallpox" wouldn't go away and accompanied him for the next few steps, then the question pounced on him and gave him a shove.

"Would you marry Ghada if she had smallpox?"

The steamship moved nearer, and a Spanish flag became visible on its mast. He gave the sea a long reproachful look and said, "How do you know that ship's not carrying handcuffs with *Made in Spain* on them?"

He tried to banish the Spanish cuffs from his walk, but they wouldn't go away. These handcuffs made a clicking noise like a slip joint knife. Slip joint knives are manufactured in West Germany. They have seven clicks, but a Spanish cuff has more. A slip joint knife moves in two directions, but the cuff moves in one direction only, strangling the wrist until the key arrives, at which point the cuff stops resisting and moves in the other direction, so the hand relaxes. Ghada's hand is different from other women's hands. There is a sort of charm in the way her slender fingers gently taper.

"Would you marry Ghada if she had smallpox?"

He looked at the steamship. The Spanish flag was fluttering in the breeze close to the shore. (That's what flags are like; they dance for any breeze on any shore.) He looked at the flag and remembered the poet Ibn al-Khatib's lament for al-Andalus.

(Those Spanish cuffs conduct the electric current. That day a man chuckled as he put the cuffs on my wrists. I couldn't make out his features

because of the blindfold pulled tight over my eyes. "Congratulations on those lovely bracelets!" he said. Then he turned and left.)

He remembered faces and names and numbers in small dingy rooms. (All of them wore Spanish bracelets like me.)

"Goddamn these Spanish cuffs," said the one they called "the uncle."

"They're better than the local ones anyway," replied the man with white hair, who was always annoying him.

"Do you think you'll get more respect if your hands have felt Spanish metal? I suppose you'll see yourself as some brave hero confronting Franco like the late, lamented Don Quixote."

"Metal, especially the metal of handcuffs, is cold wherever it's made. What annoys me about our local handcuffs is that they have specks of metal on the surface, while the Spanish ones are better polished. What's more, the local ones are heavy compared to the Spanish."

"Spanish cuffs are a blessing to be desired. We firmly believe this. When we're released we'll organize demonstrations demanding that all locally made handcuffs are replaced by Spanish ones. Did you notice that the locks on the cell doors are Italian?"

"Italy's a strong country."

"You're saying the macaroni army that was defeated in the war has grown strong?"

"Italy isn't only soldiers who like pasta more than war. It's also il duce who . . ."

Their lighthearted exchange ended up being serious. Cell 9 was laughing during their conversation, and then cell 5 joined as the discussion became heated.

It was an odd scene: locked concrete boxes getting angry, laughing, joking and then becoming involved in serious, whispered discussions.

He remembered his fellow Sagittarian talking to him about the Spanish cuffs, how they'd unfortunately lost the key, his hand had swelled up and he'd cursed the cuff's inventor.

"If his mother had pissed him out in the toilet, it would have been better for thousands of hands, not just mine."

The young man sat on a rock for a while and lit a cigarette. He stood up as the uneven surface dug into his buttocks. He brushed his hands over his trousers, picturing the reddish lumps made by the rocky teeth, a kind of short-lived smallpox.

"Would you marry Ghada if she had smallpox?"

He carried on brushing down his trousers.

Fishermen are sensible as they bring small chairs with them and carry knives with sharp pointed tips to make it easier for them to cut open the stomachs of the fish. But they are more modest than bird hunters: they put their fish in a basket — unless the basket isn't big enough, in which case they boast about their catch and show it off. Bird hunters are less bothered about the pointed tips and more concerned that their knives are sharp. They put their prey in net hunting bags or hang it on small loops at their waists, where police hang their guns. These loops are threads ending in small metal rings. If people wanted to use them as bracelets, they would have to shrink to 20 centimeters tall, and at this point a house would be a neighborhood, and a single country would be big enough for all the Earth's inhabitants.

He remembered the time he saw a hunter. The man walked like a savage conqueror who had built a gilded throne out of his victims' skulls. The little birds were bumping against his backside, dancing the indifferent dance of death, and his dog, like its owner, was wagging its tail and bragging about their large catch.

Suddenly an enormous giant reared up before the young man. *(This giant was hanging human beings alive in great nooses, hanging them randomly by their hands or necks or feet. They dance on his buttocks, while fear dances in their hearts, and they beg to be saved before they are suffocated or killed as they collide with one another).* He saw himself hanging by one hand, the other flapping in the air as he shouted, "Ghada, Ghada, Ghaaadaaa," and Ghada running breathlessly towards him but never arriving. Goddamn nightmares filling his head. *Are people born with heads full of nightmares? Who puts them there in all their different forms?*

The question pounced: "Would you marry Ghada if she had smallpox?"

In the sky not far above him he saw a small bird heading for the city.

What brought you here? Go back where you came from, little one. Look for a forest far away from the world of hunters before you become their prey.

His friend's face appeared before him.

"What's happened to you this evening?" his friend asked. "You're almost like that blind philosopher who didn't eat birds or fish. You know fish are delicious, and roast birds too."

He removed his friend so he wouldn't say anything disrespectful about the poet-philosopher, but he began to think that the smell of the sea was more alive than the smell of books.

(If only Ghada would come, and my Sagittarian friend with his girl Huda) — he remembered other friends and invited them

too — *(the sea will give us fish and plates of mezze will be served, and arak, and ice for the arak. We will spread out* The Epistle of Forgiveness, *separating its pages and putting plates of fish on them, grilled and spiced, as it should be. After we finish our meal, Ghada will be half drunk and throw some plates into the sea, unconcerned by the Sagittarian's reprimands. My Sagittarian friend will gather up the rest of the plates and tell me that Ghada will ruin my life. The two of them will laugh as he continues to scold her. A few leftovers remain on the pages of the* Epistle *still spread out on the beach. The rocks will offer al-Maʿarrī's* Epistle *to the wind, which accepts gifts from the Earth when it can carry them. It will accept the present from the rocks but will soon get bored of it, not because human beings chatter too much, but because it doesn't have time to read, as it is always busy traveling. It will throw the pages into the sea. The sea is not good at reading. It will chew the pages and give them some of its salt but be stingy with them, giving them only a little of its blueness and sending them back to shore again.*

The sea is good at reading chapters and doesn't like reading separate pages. It is good at space and blueness and is a great lover; it has loved the rocks on the shore for a long time. It woos them with patience, carrying foam from faraway places hidden in its heart and scattering it at their feet when it reaches them. It says many things to them, and they sever its tongues, but it always grows new ones so it can tell them sweet things again in the language of a sea cleansed of its saltiness, never tiring of courting them, expecting them to tease it or be angry with it, to say to it "Wait, you bastard. We'll pour a bucket of water over your head." But they are silent, their heart made of stone just like the rest of them.

If only the feast I imagined was really happening now. Friends eating, drinking, laughing. The old Arabic teacher jumps up and looks angrily at the plates on top of al-Maʿarrī's book and shouts, "Was The Epistle of Forgiveness *written for this?"*

One of the people sitting there answers somewhat recklessly, "There are plenty of copies in the market, sir," and the schoolteacher will curse this generation and go off in a fury, while al-Maʿarrī will rise from his Epistle of Forgiveness *not much bothered by the scattered pages, more bothered by those little conspiracies made by the girls on the shore with the wind, to raise their dresses and show more of their legs. Al-Maʿarrī will regretfully follow the young men's eyes shining with lust as they climb the girls' legs, and he will notice how the girls happily disregard the climbing eyes. That genius will see that some of them are too shy to urge the young men to commit more serious misdemeanors than merely looking up their skirts. But he was blind;)* — the young man suddenly remembered — *(he wouldn't see anything at all.)*

(I will go up to him and console him, indeed, heap praises on him, and tell him he is a great philosopher-poet. I'll tell him my grandmother had smallpox like him. I won't tell him my grandmother was nicer than him or that she didn't lose her sight like him, as I don't want to make him sad. I'll tell him this beach is pockmarked too, and I wish he didn't have smallpox, and I'll ask him if he's ever loved a woman and stroked her neck, for example, and I'll ask him about marriage.)

"Would you marry Ghada if she had smallpox?"

"Al-Maʿarrī is an important philosopher."

The question insisted: "Forget about him. Would you marry Ghada if she had smallpox?"

"Why would Ghada get smallpox? Isn't there still room for justice on this Earth?"

He pictured smallpox digging nasty deep pits in Ghada's soft neck. His soul cried out, and he muttered in an audible voice, "Impossible."

The question laughed. "Let's suppose—"

The young man responded excitedly, "Why not suppose that she grows a pair of wings? And that the gods emerge from legends to pour light over her head, and even over her feet?"

The question laughed sarcastically at the young man's impetuous enthusiasm.

"That could never happen. Human beings don't grow wings! And the gods sleep in ancient books and never leave them. But a human being infected with a disease like smallpox is a distinct possibility. Suppose you contracted smallpox. Would Ghada marry you?"

The young man looked at the smallpox vaccine scar on his arm and touched it with his other hand. He remembered kissing a slanting scar on Ghada's arm.

Other questions followed the big one: "Ghada might contract a disease worse than smallpox? Is the soul not afflicted with worse diseases than the body? Could she not catch pox of the soul? And would you marry her in that case?"

The questions turned the young man's head into a festival and began to leap around like grasshoppers in his festival head.

"No," said the young man calmly, thinking he had delivered a fatal blow at the leaping questions, "these are baseless assumptions."

But the main question began to argue: "Ghada is a human being, and human beings are susceptible . . . they're exposed to everything."

The young man decided to shut the roomful of questions in his head, seal it with red, white and black wax, wax of all available colors, until further notice. But as soon as the decision had taken shape, it became a corpse trampled on by dancing questions. At this he threw his cigarette into the sea, followed by all the questions rolled up into a single ball of spit, which he also aimed at the sea. As it flew through the air, a large question mark formed above it, laughing.

(The sea is not disfigured when cigarette butts are extinguished on its face. It doesn't care, and in fact it's very good at getting rid of human filth and remains beautiful and majestic. It doesn't smell its own flesh, and the cigarettes don't leave scars on its chest and buttocks and feet. A random cigarette doesn't detract from its splendor and beauty. Nobody can put chains on its wrists or blindfold it and throw it into a small dingy room.)

He cursed cigarettes and how they were stubbed out on people in small rooms. He clung onto a song that his soul had begun to weave and lost himself in its texture.

(Oh, beautiful sea, Ghada is as beautiful and splendid and childlike as you. Oh, wide sea, like my heart you are a playground for Ghada's beauty and splendor and childlike air and sweet foolishness. But you are a narcissist; your space is a playground for your own splendor and your own foolishness, so you're not like my heart. If you knew Ghada, you would abandon your narcissism and your self-absorption. One winter I will saddle you with a winter cloud the color of fire and ride on your back and lead you to the sky. We'll meet the distant god there, and He will welcome me and say, as usual, "Your horse is beautiful," and feed you the fresh clouds you love. "You comfort me in my loneliness," he will say. "Tell me what you want. Your requests will also comfort me."

"Good Lord, please change Ghada into a goddess."

"Be what you are, Ghada: a goddess," the god will say.

And she will be.

"Good Lord, turn me into a song made up of all kinds of deep joy and let me dwell in the goddess Ghada's heart."

He will say to me, "Be a song," and I will be, and he will say to the exalted Lady Ghada, "Let this song dwell in your heart, generous goddess." And she will accept.

He will look at me as I am made new in Ghada's heart and on her lips. I wander in time and space, knock on worlds and bring joy to their mournful doors.

"What's this?" he will ask me.

"This is freedom," I say.

I will see everything as I roam in the blue dome of heaven. I will descend to Earth every second. The old god will rise from his ancient seat, kick it with his luminous foot and tell himself humorously: "I've been so stupid. Couldn't I have done that before?"

He will let the world do as it pleases. He will love a woman and be transformed into a song that springs from her heart and is renewed on her lips and wanders in space. We will meet by chance in space, two songs colliding and filling the world with warm light. Hearts and dry wood will burst into leaf, and stones will say all the words they have kept hidden inside themselves for so long. We will join together and become one song that turns the world into a carnival of love. When I have become part of him, I will tell him . . .)

A gull nearby gave a shrill cry.

(Is this a good time to shriek like that? You've stolen the song, son of a bitch!)

The seagull continued to utter its shrill cry. The young man laughed at the indifference shown by the young bird towards him and his song. *(Perhaps it's protesting my song because the song forgot the sea in the sky. Why did I curse the seagull? I appear polite when I'm with other people. Polite people sometimes hide a lot of obscenities behind their polite behavior. Is it dirty to curse? Which is ruder and more obscene, wars or talking about reproduction and making love? Why have human beings chosen their genitals as a field for insults? That man who always smiles, talks in a calm and measured way, kills men, women and dreams, and wears gloves that remain shiny white after he's committed all his crimes — is he not much dirtier than a man who is good at inventing insults?)* The white-gloved man whispered, "Because all he can do is invent insults." The young man spat at him, but he kept smiling.

The seagull was still shrieking.

(Seagulls take their white color from the foam. But where does their black color come from? And why don't they take on the color of the sea and become blue? The sea is not entirely blue but tinged with green and white and many other colors that the seasons cast onto its surface. At sunset, golden and red feathers appear, all the colors of sunset dwelling in them and beautifying them.)

The young man started telling himself a story.

(Once a female seagull was pecking at her egg and a tender young beak answered her from inside the egg. The egg broke and a little seagull emerged. The father was happy because his masculinity was confirmed again, and the mother's young friends came to congratulate her. The old seagulls came to congratulate the young one and spoke with the wisdom of experience about caring for the little one and teaching him to fly and so on. After a while another whisper started up, fraught with the gulls' doubts and questions.

"A blue seagull?"

"Let's wait a few days," said a female seagull sympathetically, "and the color might change."

But the bird's blueness was becoming more obvious.

The uproar began again: "Her nightly excursions to the sea weren't in vain!"

"She seemed so quiet! Who would have thought . . ."

The young mother wept and swore by the wide horizon that she was innocent of what the rumors were claiming. Scratching his wing with his beak, an old male seagull said maliciously, "Perhaps she had cravings for sea when she was pregnant, so now the cravings are showing up like a birthmark on her child."

A kind friend who loved the mother seagull tried to throw the rumors into the sea, but her beak was incapable of picking them all up, not to mention the fact that the sea returned everything to the shore.

She continued to claim that the young mother was innocent but could do nothing in the face of the deluge of accusations, based on the blue color of the newborn, so made do with saying, "The sea raped her."

"Raped her, you say?" laughed an old female seagull. "Who knows? Maybe. I don't think anyone can have sex with a seagull unless she raises her tail for him."

"What's all the fuss about?" whispered a young seagull. "I wish a great being like the sea would love me."

The husband of the seagull whose egg had produced a blue chick perched on a faraway rock and stared into space, dry-eyed and sad. His close friends tried to cheer him up but what they said was meaningless.

"Just words," he said to himself. "They're just trying to comfort me. The truth is, she's left me." He fell silent for a long time.

The blue seagull grew up as an outsider in the land of the seagulls, and as time passed his isolation only increased and dug deeper furrows in his little heart. He couldn't hear the passing breezes whisper, "Blue seagull, beautiful blue seagull, come fly with us," because he was busy listening to his peers sniggering behind him:

"Look for your mother."

"Who knows, tonight she may sleep in the arms of the great ocean, and it will reward her with fish tasting like no other fish in the history of seagulls."

"In a while the ocean will tremble and shake and throw out its fish for the sake of her eyes."

"Or the sake of her thighs."

More raucous laughter and noisy comments.

An old male seagull passing by reprimanded them angrily.

"You bastards! May worms infest your throats and eat up your voices, and may the fish flee to the bottom of the sea and hunger gnaw at your entrails. Isn't it enough that you've lost his mother? Why do you want to kill the most beautiful seagull of you all? Pthu!*" He spits derisively.*

When the mother seagull was lost, the search revealed only the fact that she was missing. "The missing mother" was a phrase that began echoing constantly in the blue seagull's head. Flying around with his fellows was a source of torment for him and he flew alone in order not to hear "go and look for your mother" yet again. All the same, it seemed to him that everything around him was saying "go and look for your mother."

The blue seagull disappeared. There was no longer any sign of him, but much ado was made about his disappearance and the search for him. The uproar escalated and reached the press, and newspapers started competing to gather news about him. Newspaper vendors began making their rounds in the head of the lone young man who was still walking on the seashore even though darkness had fallen. They were shouting, "Latest news of the blue gull." "Don't trust fake news. Trust the truth. The Truth *newspaper gives you the facts." "Latest football results. Latest on the blue seagull.")*

The young man began to flick through the papers. In one he read, *The blue seagull has been united with his father the sea. The sea is a little bluer but only the trained eye or leading meteorology departments can determine the rise in the degree of the sea's blueness at any given moment.*

Another newspaper wrote in the introduction to a special file on the blue seagull: *(That bird unique in his color and song, who sings in the midst of shrill squawking, has spread his wings and flown away. When he was tired of flying, the evil storm threw him down on the face of an unfeeling rock. His wings were broken but he did not die. When the ants smelled his blood, they began thronging over his body, while at intervals the sea spray stung his wounds. He was incapable of either living or dying, or even committing suicide, continuing to wait for this slow progress towards death to come to an end. The rock was a cross where he suffered like no one before him.)*

The young man started flicking through a different newspaper in his head: *(A blue seagull, a cheating female and a jealous husband? Isn't this whole thing ridiculous? Can we really believe that male seagulls are jealous of their women? And if we do, how are we to believe that the sea has sex with a seagull? We're not going to bother denying these rumors that are self-evident rubbish. And the most important thing is to be aware that these rumors are being spread with the aim of distracting us from our worries and daily oppression. And for whose benefit, we wonder.)*

And in another newspaper, responding to the article in advance, the young man read, *(There are those who corrupt knowledge by the way they deliver it to us. The case is clear. They are the journalists who have an interest in the seagull's disappearance because it is in their bosses' interest. Everyone knows that with his wings and his songs he was indicating the existence of a sunny world as vast as his blueness. But the hired pens began to drop the case, making it as if he never existed, and the worst of it is that they destroy truth claiming that they serve it.)*

In the same newspaper the young man read, *(From his songs we will resurrect him, and from his resurrection we will build the world as an arena where all hearts dance with happiness. We cannot forget.)*

The young man discarded the newspaper. Papers, headlines and articles mounted up, and the noise of newspaper vendors grew louder. The young man drove it all out of his head and went on towards the city, walking faster now. He joined the crowds, crowds of people and of lights, lights that went on and off with studied regularity or stayed on all the time, and crowds of cars and air and everything. Close to the door of the cinema he saw a peanut vendor waiting for the audience to come out of the movie or the audience for the next show to arrive. He saw a youth with his hands in his pockets whistling a tune and a weary seller of lottery tickets leaning against the wall. He wanted to get inside their heads to know what they were thinking, to wish them "good evening," but he moved away from them without saying anything.

He saw a suspicious car with suspicious men sitting in it and felt afraid. The city seemed to him a ghoul who ate people and chewed them with the teeth of a cold time in small, specially designated rooms. *(The city is still a ghoul, and the cold time still chews up many people — yes people, really.)* He made for Ghada's house. *(All roads lead to Ghada this evening.)* As he approached the house, he grew less anxious and afraid. *(I hope her mother doesn't open the door with a lot of questions that don't expect answers and false expressions of welcome.)*

His fear abated completely when he pressed the bell and Ghada opened the door and said, "I knew it was you from the way you rang the bell."

He snatched a kiss. She stepped back, and he didn't know if she was scared or pleased, but she said, "Are you crazy? Here, at the door?"

He smiled.

"Good evening," he said.

When they were alone in Ghada's room, he told her about his grandmother, the beach with smallpox, Sagittarius, the Spanish bracelets, a god and a song and asked her calmly, "Would you marry me if I had smallpox?"

"Why would you have smallpox?"

"Let's suppose," he said earnestly.

"You'll never get smallpox," she replied confidently.

"What about you?" he asked her, his calmness tinged with sorrow, "Could you get smallpox?"

Fear showed in her eyes. In a shaky voice, she said, "What's got into you today?"

He was disconcerted by her question and ashamed of what he had said. She read the embarrassment on his face and smiled affectionately at him.

He told her about a blue seagull that disappeared that nobody saw anymore. She laughed and held his head close against her chest.

"Even your stupidities I can't help but love," she said.

The small room seemed like a vast space where blue seagulls and colored moons flew. Contained within the blue seagulls' songs, he saw a time that tasted of a warm dream, astonishingly beautiful. In spite of this, he felt like annoying her . . .

"I'm not stupid!"

"You sound like a small kid."

"I'm not small."

"Oh, yes you are. You're this small."

She brought her index finger close to her thumb to show him what she meant by "this small" and thrust them in his face.

He kissed the two fingers that formed the beak of a bird, possibly a seagull.

Tadmur prison, 1985.

Fattoush

Any similarity between events in this story and what actually happened in a house in Douma in Damascus on September 15, 2011, is entirely deliberate.

"Umm Sami, this is Umm Diab . . . Yes, I'm speaking from our telephone. It seems to be working again. Last night Diab visited me in a dream. He was wearing a turquoise shirt with dark blue and red stripes. He moved towards me. 'How is my lovely mother?' he asked. Before he died, he used to ask the same question when he wanted me to do something for him. I used to say, 'Be direct. Tell me what you want.' But in the dream I could only say, 'I will do anything for you. You are the light of my eyes.' He smiled his smile that melted hearts. 'I want you to make fattoush with your beautiful hands.' Then he vanished. When I woke this morning, I looked at his photo. 'I'll buy the vegetables and herbs to make fattoush,' I told him. I have just returned from the store. Please come, Umm Sami. Let us prepare and eat fattoush together."

*

The two women began preparing the fattoush for the young man who had died two months earlier. After dinner, Umm Sami wrote on her Facebook page: *My friend made delicious dishes for her son who was killed. Because of death, he forgot to turn back home.*

Later, she told Sami, her son, "I helped make fattoush for Diab, whom I never met. I know how he was killed, and I know his features from his photo."

*

Umm Sami named her son after her brother, who was arrested because of his opposition to the regime and was imprisoned in Tadmur prison in the early '80s. She imagined the meeting of the two Samis, her brother and her son. She thought of all the words they could be exchanging. About 14 years after her brother's arrest, a released prisoner visited her family to express his deepest condolences because Sami had passed away. He died without a funeral, shroud, known tomb or specific date, so he had no gravestone where she could put flowers or weep for him, and she had no chance to say her last farewell. She tried to remember the last time she had seen him when he was alive.

When Diab was shot, Umm Sami did not know his mother or his family. All she knew was that he was shot because he didn't obey the order to kneel before the president's photo. She went to console the mother of the martyr. When she saw photos, she thought that Diab looked like Sami. Many women assumed that Umm Sami was Diab's sister because she welcomed the women she didn't know, offered Arab coffee to them and sang for Diab. It sounded as if all the tenderness of the world was gathered in her song. She asked the women to release their ululations for Diab as if he were a bridegroom about to get married. She spoke about his heroism and ululated, and the women responded in kind. Umm Sami felt that Allah himself was listening to their painful celebration. The women came from different places in Damascus to show solidarity and support for the mothers of the many victims of the regime.

*

"You taught me that my son did what heroes do, but I know nothing about such things — you help me understand them. You made him alive when the others had buried him," Umm Diab said. "I love you, Umm Sami. My parents didn't give birth to a sister, but you are now my true sister."

They talked about Diab's childhood, his teenage years, his shirts, moods and many other things. They made the fattoush dish and put it on the table. While they ate, they sometimes looked at Diab's photo on the wall. It seemed as though they were eating on his behalf.

"This fattoush is the best. Diab was right to ask you to make it, thank you," Umm Sami said.

"You are welcome. As you can see, Diab doesn't eat fattoush with us. I would often make this for him, and then he would disappear with his friends."

The room became silent for a moment. The women could really feel Diab's presence.

Umm Diab broke the silence: "Umm Sami, you learned a lot of things in school, you even studied at the university. I didn't even go to elementary school. Please tell me . . . I mean, is there fattoush in heaven?"

Damascus, 2011.

An Olive Tree

I

The moment Captain Musa al-Khidr gave Sergeant Tariq Ibrahim permission to enter his office, the sergeant began talking, even before he had saluted his superior officer.

"Your village is wonderful, Captain. It has an olive tree that survived Noah's flood. Your family says hallo to you and send their greetings. Your mother said you never forget anything, and you know exactly the kind of sweets to send them, and your father said he was going to put the metal-framed bed you sent under the olive tree. 'Thank you both, and God bless you,' he said to me. Then he took hold of the edge of one of the blankets and rubbed it between his thumb and forefinger. 'These army blankets make winter disappear, Umm Musa,' he said to your mother."

"Didn't he offer you a glass of arak?"

"I drank a couple of glasses with him, but I can't keep up with him, sir. Your father — God bless him — can drink me under the table."

"The only one who can keep up with him is Abu Phoenicia. I was in tenth grade when the two of them sent me to get a three-liter bottle of arak from Abu Sa'da's shebeen. They were sitting in the shade of that olive tree you saw around noontime, and they kept drinking there till dawn next day. My father asked me whether the fact that Abel planted this tree was in my school history book. Before I could say anything, Mr. As'ad — Abu Phoenicia — said that a Phoenician princess ate an olive and spat out its stone here, and the tree grew. The beauty of this tree and the sweet air around it are because the seed from which it grew passed the lips of the Phoenician princess, he said, and if the books don't mention that it's because they and their authors are useless. The strange thing, Sergeant Tariq, is that this tree doesn't belong to anyone. One day a passerby asked Mr. As'ad, 'Who does this tree belong to?' 'The tree is free,' Mr. As'ad replied. 'Nobody owns it.' So the passerby said, 'Then it belongs to everyone,' to which As'ad replied, 'No, it owns everyone,' which put the passerby in a bad mood as he thought the whole thing was nonsense."

2

"Our friend and brother Abu Urwa, poet and great intellectual . . ."

Thus, Colonel Musa introduced the friend of his childhood and youth to his guests who had come to congratulate him on his recent promotion to colonel.

That evening Abu Urwa spoke about the olive tree.

"Its shade is unlike any other shade," he said. "The air around gives our conversations wings, and they drowse in its arms. When they awake, a delicious breeze unlike any other scatters them about, then gathers up the fragments. Our conversations hide in the air, which guards them like a treasure. We breathe our history, and the history of our ancestors, for the air here is like the beating of gentle hearts and the beating of strong hearts and resembles our souls."

The phrase "the beating of strong hearts," as Abu Urwa delivered it, sounded like the beat of the military rank being celebrated, so the audience applauded, and Colonel Musa raised a toast to "our mother the olive tree, to the air around her, and to the village of Tel al-Hawa."

Abu Urwa adjusted his spectacles and his smile and said, "Everyone who knows Tel al-Hawa knows this olive tree, for you see it wherever you are. All the houses have windows, and all the windows look out on it. It's so familiar, like the sky, and the sea in towns on the coast. The people of the desert are amazed by it . . ."

Abu Urwa's conversation, which relied on his own particular brand of eloquence and rhetoric, began to seem boring, so the colonel tried to steer the conversation in a different direction.

"Do you remember Abu Phoenicia?" he asked him.

"Who could forget him? God rest him, he used to sit with your father under that olive tree and try his best to explain the ideas of philosophers and poets and historians. Your father said to him, 'Listen, Mr. As'ad, the quivering of a woman's breast is worth all the ideas on Earth, and as far as I'm concerned, the world doesn't extend much beyond the borders of our village Tel al-Hawa, and the capital of my world is this olive tree.'

"All the same, Mr. As'ad spent the rest of his life trying to convince the people of Tel al-Hawa, and its olive tree and stones and everything else in it, of the truth of his ideas. Mr. As'ad never married, and it was Abu Ahmad, the tenant farmer, who gave him the nickname 'Abu Phoenicia' because he talked so much about the Phoenicians. He liked the name and stuck with it, to the extent that many people forgot that his name was As'ad."

Abu Phoenicia died under that olive tree. Suddenly, just like that. Three days after his death, Abu Musa poured the remains of the bottle of arak over his grave. The two of them had begun drinking it the day before he died.

3

The young men and women of Tel al-Hawa were chatting under the olive tree one evening when Amer, the second son of Musa al-Khidr, who became a Major General, stepped down from the driver's seat of a Range Rover. With him was a tall girl wearing beige cotton trousers and a white shirt patterned with brown that looked as if it had dirty marks all over it.

Basma's heart beat faster and she whispered urgently to her friend Hala, "That Italian woman has no taste whatsoever. Look at her clothes. They look as if a dog chewed them and spat them out."

Under the olive tree, Amer explained that Christine wasn't Italian but French. She had graduated with him from the School of Sculpture in Italy and, like him, had a doctorate in fine arts. Christine was clearly astonished by the sight of the huge olive tree. She said some things that nobody understood and that Amer didn't translate. Despite the tree's great age, it had never occurred to anyone to do what Christine did: She took a reel of string out of her bag, wound a length of it around the trunk, cut it and stowed it in her bag.

Basma leaned towards Hala again. "Now she's measuring the tree!" she said incredulously. "Does she think she owns the place?"

Amer looked like his uncles: a tall, handsome young man with green eyes and a thick blond beard. It was Basma who had carved the Latin letters *B* and *A* on the olive tree and claimed that Amer had done it. She wished so much that he had, just as she wished she was a little taller, and she imagined how General Musa would come in a convoy of at least three cars and ask for her hand for his son Amer.

Hala once said to her, "Why do you care about your height? Weren't you the first person from the village to get into medical school — actually, the first person from the whole area?"

Wasn't she also the only female to contribute to an art exhibition, despite the opposition of her father, who didn't want her to waste her time on this "sham" called painting? Didn't a distinguished artist say to her, "No artist in the world could paint that tree with such delicate feeling. You are a great artist. You know how to paint with your heart, not just with a brush." This had made her feel as if she could touch the clouds.

With tears in her eyes, she'd agreed: "It's true, I do paint with my heart" and added to herself, *and I carved the initials on the trunk with my heart.*

Amer handed her a handkerchief to wipe away the tears and said, "You're so sensitive! You're as generous as this olive tree . . . in a way I feel this tree binds us together!"

Why hadn't he said, "binds me to you"? He always took refuge in these ambiguous phrases. Amer had gone away and come back with this "Christine," who wrapped a rope around the trunk of the olive tree. It's a bad omen . . . except it wasn't a rope but rather a string any child could cut. *Who's going to tell her our tree isn't measured by rope or string, but by our hearts full of love? I hate her. But she's tall, and her eyes are beautiful.* All the same, I don't think Amer has the right to say to her, "Your eyes are the color of the leaves on this tree."

4

Old Abu Musa's eyes filled with tears when he heard his grandson, Mazen, exclaiming to his mother, "The tree's corpse is huge, Mum!"

The word *corpse* upset his mother, but, stripping off his dirty blue shirt, the boy continued.

"They've shaved off her hair, so now she's a bald corpse!" He threw his shirt down on a green plastic chair. His mother was crying again. She cried when she saw the tree falling down. She carried on peeling a grilled eggplant, trying in vain not to look at the place where the olive tree used to be. It had left behind a huge void.

"Why are you crying, Mum?"

She looked at her son's face thinking of the cruel way he had described the uprooted tree. She looked at the fuzz that was starting to darken on his upper lip. Ignoring his question, she said reprovingly, "You're not a child anymore. How did your shirt get so dirty?" Then looking at the shirt lying on the chair, she went on, "And that's no place to put it."

Tears came into Abu Musa's eyes again as he looked at the uprooted trunk of the olive tree. His images of it, the words he used to describe it, stayed in his memory and on the sides of the glass he drank from, and he walked in the olive tree's funeral procession with his head bowed, the air above his head transformed into a coffin.

That evening he said to Umm Musa, "She's dead. My last friend."

"What about me? Don't I mean anything to you?"

He replied with a sad smile, "You are my first love and my last."

When old Abu Masa learned his son Musa al-Khidr had a hand in digging up the olive tree, he made the journey to see him, intending to say to him, "If I'd pissed you onto a pile of stones, it would have been better than giving birth to you. Were you the one who cut down the olive tree? And such a glorious olive tree!"

But when he arrived, he merely said, "What a pity! The most beautiful olive tree in the world has been killed."

5

Three months after General Musa retired, Abu Urwa visited him. The general welcomed him warmly and reproached him for not visiting sooner. When the two men sat down to drink tea with lemon, General Musa al-Khidr said, "What I love most in this villa is the wooden bench I'm sitting on now. Amer and my French daughter-in-law worked on it constantly for six months straight to make it like this. After they had finished carving it, Christine named it 'The Scent of Tel al-Hawa.' It's the trunk of that olive tree that used to be on the street. See how beautiful the veins in the olive wood are? The Minister of Culture told me that joining pieces of wood together requires great craftsmanship, and he was amazed when I told him that the bench was made of a single piece of wood."

"But it's dead. And the olive tree was alive."

"What do you mean? Have you come to insult me in my own home?"

Abu Urwa stood up and left the villa as if he was walking in the olive tree's funeral procession again. He decided to write an elegy that would be recited by all the people of Tel al-Hawa. He told himself that it was going to be the most important poem he would write in his entire life.

Damascus, 2009.

A Shipwreck

I

Before he saw the bag, he was walking slowly on the sand, not noticing how the sea erased his footmarks or how his shoes made new marks in the sand, unconcerned by the sea's actions.

He didn't know why he'd come to the seashore. Depression, a feeling of claustrophobia and a gloomy sense of alienation mingled in a song saturated with bitterness. He tried in vain to free himself from its endless melodies. They distracted him, melted his soul in their heartbreaking sounds and carried him to the seashore. The song seemed to want him to escape from it. As he continued to walk aimlessly along the sand, he suddenly saw an old sailor's sack.

The man descended from the wings of the song, shook it off as best he could and went over to the sack. He took it in his hands and ran his fingers tenderly all over it.

"The sea threw you out one day with its usual indifference," he said.

He opened it and emptied its contents onto the sand and began inspecting them with interest: a photo yellowed by time in a way that didn't suit the face of the woman hidden within it, who had preserved the freshness of her smile despite everything; a pipe that should have been retired and placed respectfully in a box of memories long ago; a pack of 52 cards, clearly miserable as it was missing its jokers.

"Its owner must have inherited it from an old sailor," muttered the man as he examined the frayed edges of the sack, empty now except of its dampness. The past was hiding in the tattered sack like a dumb ostrich burying its head in the sand.

"We are both strangers and friends," said the man to the discarded sack.

It said nothing, lying there silently like a small weary dog.

The man became a child playing a game of clairvoyant and seashells. In clairvoyants' eyes, cowrie shells are tongues telling you a story about your future.

The man who was no longer walking, the man who sat down on the sand, spread the playing cards and the photo of the woman and the pipe on the ground in front of him, then gathered them up, and they grew tongues that told him an old story.

2

A ship arrived at the entrance to a rocky channel. Shortly after it had entered the channel, the sailors were reduced to crying desperately for help, seeking deliverance from an unknown place. Their eyes scanned possible places in vain. One sailor remembered the happy days he had spent in their last port of call and wept bitter tears to himself because the happy days to come were going to be erased by death. Another sailor was smoking his pipe just before the uproar began and he fixed his eyes on the raging sea in an attempt to drive it back, but it was no use. So he placed his pipe in his bag and appeared to be at peace, but underneath his calm exterior smoldered volcanoes of anxiety and sorrow.

3

The distracted man on the sandy beach arranged the playing cards in the shape of a ship. He made the pipe into a mast, and the photo of the smiling woman into a flag on top of the mast. Then he muddled them all up again.

4

There, in the place where the sea sprouted teeth — even though they were black and rotten they were capable of destroying ships and sailors' lives — the ship was wrecked and transformed into a tribe of the dead whose children argued with one another, some of them migrating to the bottom of the sea and others continuing to float on the surface.

The waves, who were holding a noisy celebration, found a floating shipwreck, and in the midst of their party they had enough time to brush their teeth on it and toss it to and fro.

5

Something happened that nobody was expecting. The storm said the music of death it was whistling would not leave a single member of the ship's crew alive, and the waves said they loved to dance to the music played by the storm. A distant sun appeared from behind a black cloud. It wept tears spun from warm glowing gold and said with a mother's sadness: "Not one of them will survive." The ship rose and fell on the dancing waves, changed to a frightened heart that played its terror like a drum in this festival of death and then was wrecked on the teeth of the rocky channel.

But something else happened that nobody was expecting: the ship's captain escaped death. He fought with the storm and the waves like a skillful acrobat, playing among "the wild leopards of death the salt water hid in its heart," as Abu al-Mish, a sailor from the ship, described them. The captain did not tame the waves but snatched his life from their jaws. Nimbly he climbed up one of the rocks in the "channel of curses," his name for it. He was wounded by the rock and bled profusely but called it "the rock of life." He was tired and fell asleep in the arms of the storm, the waves and the rock — the rock where his ship was wrecked.

6

His hunger and thirst awoke with him as soon as he opened his eyes. Salt water kindled small fires in the captain's inflamed wounds. While his eyes were still closed, a wave appeared and raised its head above the rock where he was sleeping. It made a bet with the rock that he wasn't just asleep but in a coma, then melted away before the bet was settled.

"The rocks speak slowly, suffer quietly, receive the relentless slaps of the waves with a stern face and quarrel with them frequently. The grains of sand swallow the water and scare the waves into retreating of their own accord." So said the man and stared again at the playing cards spread before him and the pipe and the smiling photo of the woman.

7

The captain looked with tired eyes at the sea, which was still a vast arena for the waves' rousing dance to the flutes of the storm.

"You two deserve to be hanged," said the captain, indicating the sea and the storm with his eyes. "Why all this joy and excitement over the corpse of a poor ship?"

The storm carried on whistling inside the great shells it formed from the body of the void. The sea remained undecided whether to be valleys or mountains, so a mountaintop suddenly became a valley bottom. Among its valleys and mountains, the sea was a legendary dragon, white foam flying from its thousands of mouths, showing its anger.

On the crest of a big wave, the captain saw the remains of his ship: ropes, rubber tires and some wooden crates, but they were soon gone.

"Only I know what it means for a captain to stand and look at the wreckage of his ship." He didn't know whom he was addressing. For the first time, he had a profound sense that it wasn't right that ships were wrecked. His soul hovered around the shattered remains, fluttered above them and plunged into the depths to talk to the wheelhouse, the sailors' bodies, the fuel tank and whatever else was there. He pleaded with what tenderness he possessed.

"Let's go back to how we used to be: a crew, a ship and a captain." He thought this was convincing enough, but nobody was convinced. He even begged the sailor Abu al-Mish to wake up. "But the dead don't wake up," he said regretfully and didn't dare to add, "If only they'd all wake up except Abu al-Mish." But this last sentiment was buried in remote parts of his soul, covered up by his love for the ship and all the sailors.

8

The captain did not climb the rock of life-death alone. He carried part of the past with him, a heavy sack containing many people, places and events he had known. Abu al-Mish fought time, and it came with him to the rock. The huge waves were unable to erase the faces, events and places. There was nothing the captain could do about that, but he would have liked to say it's sometimes unfortunate that we humans possess the faculty of memory. Abu al-Mish's simple words lashed him like a whip: "We must sail northeast!" These plain words turned into prickly thorns, and the captain searched for them in the blood still seeping from his wounds and was finally convinced they remained hidden there, in the blood yet to flow.

A cloud passing over the sea spoke up, telling him his blood was evaporating due to the heat of his pain, and the red colors in the sky were made up of blood evaporating from human wounds. But the sea roared angrily, "You idiot! How often have I told you that the bloodshed you see in the sky at sunset is the blood of the sun slaughtered every day by what it witnesses on Earth, and that the red in the eastern sky every day is the blood of childbirth, a daily senseless birth from the womb of yesterday's pain?"

The cloud was angry at the sea for reprimanding him and reminded him that he disliked the blood the sun spread over him morning and evening, and had to bathe frequently to wash it off.

The captain did not hear this conversation and couldn't see the angry cloud drifting away towards the plains. He was busy begging Abu al-Mish to extract the thorns from his blood, to forgive him.

9

When Abu al-Mish entered the captain's cabin, he tried to bury his anxiety in the fingers holding his pipe. The anxiety spread through the air around him along with the pipe smoke.

"Good evening, Captain."

"Good evening."

The captain didn't want to remember, but he couldn't stop himself. After Abu al-Mish entered his cabin, he felt the air he was breathing grow heavy.

After a brief silence he asked, "What do you want, you devil?"

"I want to save the ship." Abu al-Mish spoke the words calmly, closing his left eye slightly as usual. The slightly closed eye seemed to shine more fiercely. The captain looked at him suspiciously, then turned away.

"This troublesome brat is here again to say the ship has two captains! As far as I know, a ship should only have one captain, its official captain, and this secret captain who's trying to take over must be gotten rid of. For a ship to travel safely, it must have only one captain. But he's a devil who claims to be a good man. He thinks his fine words will make the sailors trust him. They think he's a good man and . . . if he deserved to be captain, he wouldn't have spent his life as a mere sailor. I became a captain because of all my hard work. I won't let this bird of ill omen ruin the ship."

(The captain was looking away and didn't see Abu al-Mish's soul pouring from his eyes and lips, and spreading through the air, creating a warm world that embraced sailors on board all the ships in the world.)

The sailor was still looking at the captain, who broke his silence and said, "What are you going to save the ship from, you gloomy owl?"

"From a storm that I can smell with every cell in my body. The approaching hurricane may strike us in this rocky channel. We must sail northeast today and tomorrow. Then we can continue on our way."

For no apparent reason as far as Abu al-Mish could see, the captain said sarcastically, "You can put your northeast up your ass. How about we turn our ship's timbers back into trees and shelter in their shade? Is this what sailors are like?"

"Listen to me, Captain. The storm will awaken the wild leopards of death that lurk in the heart of the salt water. To them our ship will look no bigger than a little rabbit, so . . ."

"All you can do is moan. Why did you become a sailor? Why didn't you get a job as a preacher in one of those houses of incense and candles? You don't even deserve to sit on a beach and look at the sea. You should have been a lizard in the desert."

In a calm voice, as if he were not addressing the captain, Abu al-Mish said, "I've spent my life at sea. Hot blood can burn the hot-blooded. Neither the sea nor the storm can measure the temperature of blood. In love, it's a wonderful thing to burn and shine like a sun. But seas are a different matter. It's true that the sea will not cease to exist if a ship is wrecked. There will always be the sea, sailors and ships, but this doesn't mean that your ship will be wrecked. The sea is stupid and does as it pleases, and the captain should not be like the sea."

The captain's voice was full of anger, an anger that showed in his eyes as he shouted, "That's enough of your stupid advice and gloomy preaching. Take care you don't infect the sailors with your talk of storms and death. I'm the captain here, not you!"

"I can hear you when you speak quietly," said Abu al-Mish. All the same, he raised his voice as he went on, "I want to be buried on dry land even though I've given my life to the sea. I don't want to be buried deep down in its cruel waves. Don't be foolish. One act of foolishness can cost a lifetime."

"I promise to relieve my ship of your cowardly heart and throw you out like a stray dog at the first port we come to."

"That's if we reach a port. Once again, don't be stupid, Captain!"

The captain's anger grew. He clenched his fist, extending his forefinger and making his fist like a gun, stabbing the air with the forefinger-gun barrel. Tiny insects, hardly visible, flew out of his mouth with the letter *T* as he pointed to the door shouting, "Out-t-t!"

10

As Abu al-Mish emerged from the captain's cabin, he looked up at a dark cloud and read on its face a prophecy of his future: "This is your final voyage." He repeated what he had said to the captain: "The sea, sailors and ships will always be there." Then he looked beyond the cloud at a faraway place above the sea.

"How stupid I am. Why did I say I wanted to be buried on dry land? Does a dead man care about his grave? But I would really like to be buried away from the sea, and I want to have a tombstone. One day a woman will read on the tombstone: *Here lies the sailor Abu al-Mish*, and then I will rise from the sea. Did I say the sea? I will rise from the grave. She will laugh at the sight of me as I brush the dust off my shroud. I will ask the worms of death to hide so I don't scare her. 'Haven't you had enough of life, sailor?' she will ask me. 'Can anyone have enough of life, blessed woman?' I will say to her. It would be wonderful if she planted a rose by my grave with flowers that looked like ships. A rose planted by a woman would keep me company in my death. I would even rise from the grave to search for her, but I would never reach dry land. If only they would put up small signposts pointing to the sea and telling people, *Here lies Abu al-Mish*."

Abu al-Mish coughed and gazed at the sea nearby.

"Don't be stupid like the captain of our ship. Why be careless just because he is? So because of the recklessness of a captain an old friendship is ruined. You know I can't live without you. But I don't want you to destroy me because you are my friend."

The sea seemed like a forbidding priest and the ship a confessional. Abu al-Mish was awestruck as he made his confession, mixed with a prayer of supplication: "You know that I cannot live without you. My life would be empty without you, sea. I was created for you and have lived with you for a long time, and because I trust you and fear you, I will open my heart to you. When I am with you I long to reach dry land, the women in its ports, its cafes and its long streets. But when we stay on land for long, we feel lost and homeless there. We feel you in our blood. So between land and sea, between sea and land, we wander all our lives. Please give me another chance to wander like this!"

11

One day when he arrived in port, a woman presented Abu al-Mish with a pipe, a pack of cards and her photo. He fell in love with her and her city by the sea. The port where he first looked into her eyes was the most beautiful of all the ports, and the journey there made his heart fly over the ship and outrun it. He had always wished the ship could swallow up the sea and just like that reach its destination.

"What were you doing?" he asked her after he arrived.

"I was waiting," she said with an enchanting smile. Then he wished he could hold her forever.

In his cabin, Abu al-Mish sat smoking dreams and memories with a pipe a woman had given him. Some of his memories were about her, and as he smoked his anxiety was plain to see. All of this mingled with the tobacco smoke billowing from the ancient pipe and swirled around in the air of his cabin.

He took the photo of the woman out of his old sack.

"On this piece of paper, you can keep your smile forever."

Why did she agree to go away with him? (He meant with death.) It seemed to him that she had died long ago.

"God who is just will give us a little room on the seashore in His paradise, and we will travel together in a ship fitted by an angel who is excellent at fitting ships. God will not forget that He is just . . ."

The old man smelled death approaching and heard the shrieks of the sailors. Calmly he finished smoking his pipe and then returned it to the ancient sack. He wrapped the woman's photo in a plastic bag, put it beside the pipe and closed the sack. He opened his cabin door and smelled with every cell in his body the dark hours of terror, the scent of death growing stronger, the omens of the storm containing only gloomy prophecies. The old man began to fight with himself.

"Why didn't I talk to the sailors? Why didn't I tell them that shipwreck and death awaited them if we didn't make the captain go back on his stupid decision? Why didn't I tell them? They were dreaming of gifts they would buy in the next port to take to those waiting for them in other ports. Why didn't I tell them? The women on shore will tire of waiting so long. Their children will search in vain for the missing men. Why didn't I tell them? Have I become less hot-blooded? The captain can't do a thing when the crew says no. It's no longer any use if I say there's a storm approaching, for we are in the hands of the storm now. All I can do is hope for something that seems impossible: that we manage to get through this rocky channel. All I can do is hope. What's left for the sailors to do? They must fight to resist death. Talking to them now is only a waste of time. Why didn't I talk to them before?"

12

The captain is still alone on the rock of life (which is also the rock of death). Abu al-Mish emerges from the wave. A shark leaps up and bites off his arm. Small fish jump around in the waves, fighting over their share of his eyes. Some of his bones have become visible. Fish have carved a boat from his thigh. Fresh blood flows from the places where sea creatures feed. Thousands of monkeys emerge from Abu al-Mish's eyes and laugh along with him.

"Are you going to throw me out like a dog at the next port?"

The captain tries not to see. He recites a short incantation to exorcise Abu al-Mish.

"Blessed be your soul, sailor. It was right that you died."

Abu al-Mish chortles, his laughter mingling with the clamor of his sea monkeys, the hissing of the captain's hunger, the sounds of thunder in the sky and the howling of a storm still in its infancy. The captain puts his head in his hands and presses hard, trying to smother his memory.

No sooner has the captain forgotten Abu al-Mish than he emerges again like a missile from the crest of a big wave, tracing a straight line up into the air and rapidly descending in a spiral movement. The sailor gathers up his limbs from the bellies of the fish, retrieving his foot from a ferocious fish that likes feet because their taste reminds it of something in particular. Abu al-Mish puts his eye back upside down. He sticks his flesh onto his bones any old way: skin to the inside and severed veins leaking blood to the outside. His face is a doughy mix of bloody flesh. He stands before the captain with his new look. The captain closes his eyes. The sailor laughs.

"You must close your ears, too, Captain, but they don't close. Ears are different. In my case, there's no longer any difference between one part of me and another, and you've abandoned yourself to loneliness and imminent death. You're going to feed the fish, Captain. Maybe that sweet girl Mattia you met in the last port will eat the fish that ate you. They'll be rotten fish if they've eaten your head. In any case you'd be lucky to pass through her lips, even if it's when she's spitting you out. I don't know if you'd be so lucky if Mattia ate the fish and flushed you down the . . . ha . . . ha . . . ha." Abu al-Mish continued to laugh, accompanied by his monkeys, the storm and the black clouds. "Why are you sad, Captain? There will always be the sea, sailors and ships."

The captain becomes an echo of the words of Abu al-Mish the sailor. He sees the sailor scattered over the sea in the face of the storm: *There will always be sea, sailors, and ships.* The echo resounds deep in the captain's body, causing cracks to break out in it which he tries to suppress.

13

When the captain woke from his trance, he saw ships moving in all directions, quickly, slowly, big ships, little ships, and there among them he saw his own ship. He was like a mother catching sight of the child everyone had said was dead.

"Good morning," he said to the ship. "It's her!" he shouted to himself. "The mast, the colors, the rust, everything says it's her. And at the top of the mast is the sailor Abu al-Mish. It's her for sure."

The captain waved, weary, hungry and unexpectedly joyful. He was almost jubilant when he noticed Abu al-Mish looking at him from the top of the mast.

"Hey sailor! You're a sailor, not a flag. Why are you standing on the mast like that? Throw me a rope!"

The old man threw down one end of the rope and began to play with the captain as if he were a cat. Every time the captain jumped to pick up his end of the rope, the old man moved it out of his reach. This exhausted the captain and left him with nothing but handfuls of salty water that quickly ran through his fingers, but he carried on with the game. With a skillful leap, he managed to grab the end of the rope, at which point the old man threw the other end into the sea and sailed on.

The captain looked away and still saw the ship, Abu al-Mish on the mast and himself, a disappointed cat. He looked all around, trying to avoid the sight, but everywhere he looked he saw Abu al-Mish on the ship's mast. When he looked at the sky, he saw the ship and even with his eyes closed he saw Abu al-Mish letting go of the other end of the rope.

"Impossible. The ship was wrecked. I saw the wreckage with my own eyes."

"Where's the wreckage, Captain?" yelled Abu al-Mish from the top of the mast.

He stared as hard as he could, trying to see the shipwreck again, but all he could see was his moment of failure on the bare rocks. The rock appeared unconcerned by all the noise, bathed in lethal silence and calm in this festival of death.

"The ship is alone now, consumed by loneliness. The sailors are alone, consumed by the chill of death. The ship has sailed away, like a wounded pigeon tossed to and fro by mischievous children, as one wave passes it on to the next."

He himself felt like a miserable child attacked by a gang of vicious boys who stole his ball and passed it to one another as they ran away from him.

"Waves are a gang of toughs who steal ships and treat them like footballs, playing with them on the surface of the salty water."

He stared expectantly into the distance but couldn't make out a single familiar port.

"Why don't the ports come and save us? We're the ones who saved them from exile and ruin. If it weren't for us, they'd just be deserted beaches, destroyed by random events." He sat down despondently. "Ports are only good for devouring us and our ships' cargoes."

The image of the ship remained, plowing through the waves with Abu al-Mish at the top of its mast.

"He's looking at me and laughing. I didn't know this was how people were raised from the dead. Is there something funny about death, Sailor?"

But the sailor didn't answer. He was too busy laughing.

14

The captain grew tired of standing and staring, tired of sitting, tired of closing his eyes, tired of everything. He cursed the sea and the storm, cursed being saved from a shipwreck and cursed the moment when it occurred to humans to produce ships.

Abu al-Mish appeared, still chuckling. The captain saw the sailor's lips trying to say something.

"He must want to tell me I'm a dirty barrel of curses."

He could see the weariness of the days to come, their pain and the abiding presence of Abu al-Mish. He cursed them and lashed out at them and the sea and the storm and all the boats, but he didn't hit any of them, so he kicked his life on the back of the head, and it fell into the sea.

15

In a city by the sea, on the wall of a room in a little house, hung a frayed sailor's sack. A young man wrote on the sack with his finger, *Here lies Abu al-Mish the Sailor*, but the writing was invisible and quickly vanished in the air.

Tadmur prison, 1985.

The Two Nasties

Twenty-three years ago, Mr. Badr pushed his glasses up on his nose and shouted at me and Bassam, "What are you doing, you nasty boys?"

Then he asked me angrily, "How can you give him gum straight from your mouth?"

"I only gave him half," I said softly.

He looked at me in disgust and continued to shout.

"You tore it in half with your dirty fingers and then shared your germs and filth with him." Turning to Bassam, he said with mounting fury, the spit flying from his lips, "And you, how can you agree to take gum from somebody else's mouth?" Then he added for good measure, "And when will you learn not to wipe your nose on your shirtsleeve?"

When the teacher left I said to Bassam, "Did you see how his moustache danced as he told us off?"

"It dances all day long," said Bassam, "because he's always shouting, damn him and his moustache. I don't like Mr. Badr or his belly or his spectacles." He paused for a moment then said, "In fact, I don't like school."

The matter did not end there. Some of the students actually enjoyed the teacher insulting us, and even though they shared their gum just like Bassam and me, they decided to tease me, calling me "the first nasty" instead of my real name, Salem, which was after my grandfather. Bassam and I had a few fights with them, and then they came up with another way of annoying us and began saying the word *nasty* whenever we were around them. When we were with Fayiz, the shortest student in our class, he turned to address the other students:

"Do you know what the word *nasty* means in the dictionary?"

I ignored the provocation, but Bassam confronted Fayiz angrily, speaking in his usual hoarse voice:

"The dictionary says you're a son of a bitch."

Fayiz made fun of Bassam's lisp, so Bassam threw him to the ground and carried on insulting him, planting his shoe on the short boy's neck.

*

Bassam and I continued to share a seat up until the ninth grade, and when I passed the exams and he failed, we parted ways. I went on to high school, and he stayed in middle school, but we continued to exchange shirts and secrets. Most of our secrets were related to his unrequited love for Ghada. He was fascinated by her laughter and her black hair.

"Her hair flies in the air like a horse's mane, and I can't stop myself looking at her," he told me once.

"So you've joined the long line of Ghada's lovers, which means almost all the boys in the school," I commented, to his annoyance.

We were reconciled when I confessed to him that I was in love with Maysun, and she had asked me not to write dedications to her on the books I gave her, because if I did, she would cross them out so nobody could see them.

"She's right," he laughed. "You don't have to philosophize. Love can't bear philosophy."

Bassam left school the day Ghada got engaged, when she was in ninth grade. He had a fight with the skinny science teacher and punched him on the nose and was expelled. Before his 18th birthday, he found work in the vegetable market. He told me he was employed by the intelligence services to keep a record of what people said and that nobody else must know. This caused a rift in our relationship, as I didn't want to be friends with someone who spied on people's thoughts and made trouble for them.

*

Seventeen years ago, a wedding took place in our village, the likes of which the village had never known. Ghada was marrying a young merchant from Damascus, and the groom wanted the wedding to be in our village. He came with a fleet of cars carrying more passengers than the entire population of the village, in addition to varieties of food and sweets that our kitchens had not seen before. This was also the first time a cake had been cut with a Damascene sword on the village threshing floor where wedding celebrations were usually held in the village. The wedding coincided with the release of the results of the high school exams, and despite the cooling off of relations between us, Bassam visited me the following day to congratulate me on my success.

"Where were you during the wedding?" I asked him.

He looked uncomfortable and replied quickly that he had been busy. Then he asked me if I would be going to the Military Academy in Homs to train to be an officer. I assured him that I would hate to be a soldier and take orders.

"So what are you going to study?"

"I'd like to study law."

"There are more law students than there are stars in the sky."

"I'm going to add to their huge number. What are you going to do?"

"I'm 18 now. I'm going to apply for a job in the intelligence services." As he left, he said sarcastically, "We'll see if a university degree is any use to you."

*

There weren't huge numbers of students in the law faculty despite what Bassam had said, and my days studying there were among the best of my life.

*

Fifteen years ago, Maysun enrolled in the Faculty of Law at Damascus University, and I helped her find a room in al-Shaykh Saad, the neighborhood where I rented part of an old building. Most evenings we had dinner together, and most mornings I used to accompany her to the university even if I didn't have classes. We weren't the only couple, of course. We got to know a number of students, but we were closest to Manal and Ashraf. One of our colleagues in the Faculty of Law called us "the doves" because we usually wore white shirts. I was with Manal in third year, Ashraf was in fourth year and Maysun was still a new student in first year. Maysun once said during a gathering of the doves in my room that many people form relationships, but true lovers are few. Manal assured us that Ashraf had said the same thing. This led us on to a discussion about love and the conditions needed for it to flourish and bloom. Ashraf recited a poem by Lorca. We were greatly affected by the story of the poet's execution when he faced the firing squad wearing a white shirt and reciting a poem:

What is a person without freedom, Mariana? Tell me. How can I love you if I am not free? Can I give you my heart if it is not mine?

We talked a lot, but that story and that poem and the image of the poet in his white shirt were among the many factors that drew me emotionally to search for freedom. I continued to be fascinated by the story even though I realized that the only real thing in it was that Lorca had actually been executed by a firing squad made up of Franco's fascist forces.

*

Six years ago, I met Ashraf and we talked about the need for us as lawyers to establish an association dedicated to promoting respect for laws and human rights. Ashraf repeated a truth I knew only too well: "Where dictatorship prevails, laws and freedoms are abused." The words of the Spanish poet, *How can I love you if I am not free?*, continued to be more compelling.

Six years ago, I began my three months of activism against the violations of people's right to free speech. After those three months, I was arrested from my office, which my wife Maysun had patiently furnished with purchases from the used furniture market, managing to make it look luxurious.

Six years ago, I was taken by force to the branch of the intelligence services known as the State Security Branch. I heard a voice that awakened memories of the village school, Mr. Badr and the chewing gum I'd torn in half to give to Bassam. I heard Bassam's voice. I was convinced that it was his, the same hoarseness and lisp. Bassam was a torturer being asked by the interrogator to loosen my tongue so that I would name those involved in subversive activity (as he called it). The torturer replied, "Sir, this piece of shit can't endure a beating."

When the interrogator left, Bassam was foaming at the mouth and spitting out words I didn't understand after he had punched me on the nose and my blood ran down over my chest and white shirt. I gathered from his furious, incoherent talk that I was a traitor. I pictured Mr. Badr's moustache dancing as he called us "nasty boys," scolding us as the spit flew from his mouth.

*

A week ago, I was released. On the day of my release, I left our house in Damascus with my wife, to stay with our family in the village. Among the first to visit me there was Bassam's mother. This lady in her seventies hugged me, telling me I was like her son Bassam. Many people visited me that day to congratulate my family on my safe release and to observe the effects of prison on me. One of these visitors was Mr. Badr.

His moustache had drooped, and he did not remind me of the chewing gum incident. Instead, he praised my hard work when he was my teacher. When everyone had left I told my wife about Bassam, my childhood friend, and Mr. Badr and the punch that made my blood flow in the interrogation room. Maysun was visibly moved. She hugged me and said to me, "Write something."

*

Yesterday, I wrote this.

Tadmur prison, 1986.

The First Kiss

I

Taima: May 27, 2012

The miracle happened. We were alone together in the house. When I moved close to him, expecting us to exchange the first kiss, the one he'd promised before he was arrested, I thought the tears welling up in his eyes were tears of joy. The day he was released my heart was dancing with joy, along with the trees, the clouds and the wind, and I wished I could make the whole city beautiful. But we didn't embrace. He was sobbing as if his soul was breaking in pieces.

"Don't be sad, Taima," he said through his tears.

Before I could reply, my brother, Salem, came through the front door carrying bags full of vegetables and fruit. The smell of apricots reached my nose. It usually made me happy, but not today.

2

Taima: April 13, 2012

I was startled by my mother's voice coming unexpectedly from behind me.

"What are you doing on the balcony all the time?"

I turned to look at her, and she repeated, frowning, "I asked you what you're doing here."

"I'm . . . nothing . . . I'm not doing anything. Just watering the plants."

"How many times a day do you water them?"

"I'm not watering them. I mean I don't water them all at once. I water them one by one . . . each time . . . I mean."

I was scared my mother might have spotted Yamen on his balcony opposite.

3

Umm Salem: April 18, 2012

I noticed my daughter Taima was spending a lot of time on the balcony, and as I watched her, I realized she had grown up. She did her hair carefully or tied it back in a scarf, taking care she looked nice before she went onto the balcony, and she would rush out impatiently as if her heart was planted there. I saw her burying things in the flowerpots and gesturing to someone. So she had grown up, but if her father or brother found out, God knows what curse would befall her. From the kitchen window I saw Yamen exchanging signs with her. They waved awkwardly at each other as if they were doing something illegal and blew frightened kisses in the air.

"What are you planting in the earth there?" I asked her.

"Seeds. Seeds to give us beautiful flowers."

When she went to school, I dug up the pots and took out one of those seeds. I removed the plastic wrapping around it and uncovered a piece of paper with sweet words written on it but no names, just a heart in place of a signature. Taima had grown up, but she was still a child.

4

Yamen: April 18, 2012

My father called me when I was on the balcony.

"Yamen, what are you doing there?"

"What do people usually do on balconies, Dad? I'm smelling God's pure air."

"I know exactly what you're smelling. Come inside and concentrate on your studies."

My father was bad at pretending to be angry. He was obviously smiling behind his unconvincing stern expression. I went into my room and began writing a letter to Taima. I felt awkward writing the first love letter of my life, embarrassed by my sense that the phrases in my head weren't appropriate for Taima and by my fear that my father would burst into the room and read what I was writing. I wrote a lot, crossed out a lot and finally wrote this short message: *I wish God would lend me his eraser, so I could rub out the distance between our balconies.*

I didn't sign my name, just drew a small heart, folded the piece of paper and put it in my pocket ready to give to Taima the next day. From then on I wrote a letter every day, without mentioning her name or mine.

5

Taima: April 19, 2012

"Taima, stop. Don't move!" shouted my brother. Then he pounced on my hand like a bird of prey, forced my fingers open and prized out Yamen's message, which I hadn't finished reading even though it was short.

"We'll sort this out at home," he said furiously, and when we reached home, he took the belt off his trousers and attacked me like a wild animal. Dodging his blows as best I could, I begged my mother to protect me. She swore at me before she knew why my brother was attacking me, and when he waved the little piece of paper in my face, she said as if she knew the whole story.

"Is it a letter from that bastard, Yamen? Have I given birth to a child who will cover us in shame?"

"I haven't done anything," I protested to my mother.

"Shut up," she said to me, then yelled in my brother's face, "Go to your room!"

"But she—" began my brother angrily.

"I said get out!" repeated my mother. She grabbed me by the hand and dragged me into her room, closed the door and began scolding me. "Are you crazy or stupid? Did we send you to school so you could learn to read love letters? Did you write letters to him too?"

"No."

"Liar!"

"I swear to God."

"Okay. Listen. Your father will find out about this, and I don't know what he's capable of. Listen to me, you stupid girl! Don't try to make him angry. God alone knows what he'll do."

When my father came home, my brother held the letter out to him.

"Here you are," he announced loudly. "Look at the love letters your daughter's been receiving!"

As my father took the letter I wished the ground would swallow me up. I couldn't keep my head bowed and looked at him surreptitiously as he read the letter. When he raised his eyes and put the letter in his pocket, I bowed my head again. He went over to the fridge and poured himself a glass of water, then headed for the guest room, calling me in a firm, calm voice: "Taima, come here."

I followed him as if I was going to my grave.

"Close the door," he said, and I closed it as if I was never going to open it again.

My father read the letter aloud:

"'*I'll do everything I can to deserve your love, and to earn a kiss from you. It will be the first kiss in my life.*' Look at me," he ordered, as I cringed with embarrassment before him.

I raised my eyes obediently and he asked, "Who gave you this letter?"

Barely whispering, I answered, "Yamen."

"How did he get it to you?"

"He asked to borrow a chemistry book and he put it inside the book."

"But he's in the class above you. Why did he borrow a textbook from you?"

"I don't know."

Did my father smile, or did I just want him to smile?

"Listen, daughter. Your reputation is our reputation. Don't make us a subject of gossip."

"Okay."

When my father stroked my hair kindly, I burst into tears.

In the calm, firm voice he had used the whole time, he said, "Don't cry. Send your brother Salem to me."

6

Taima: April 23, 2012

On the way back from school, we passed a demonstration. Many people were taking part in it, including our physics teacher. With my own eyes I saw them arresting my brother Salem, then Yamen, and tying their hands behind their backs underneath their backpacks. I felt they were ripping my heart out of my chest and throwing it in the Grand Cherokee along with my brother and my love. This was the first time I'd called him that to myself after I'd suppressed these thoughts in order to preserve what my father called my "reputation." I ran home and was almost knocked over by a taxi as I crossed the street in front of the entrance to our building. There was a cacophony of sounds: the taxi driver hooting and shouting, and my mother calling out to me as she caught sight of me from the balcony. She was waiting for me at the door in her pistachio-green dress.

"Are you crazy?" she shouted.

"They've arrested Yamen and Salem," I replied, bursting into tears.

My mother struck her chest repeatedly. "They've arrested Salem? No! No!" she wailed. Then she ran to the phone and called my father. "A disaster," I heard her saying.

I'd mentioned Yamen's name first, before my brother's, and my mother hadn't punished me.

7

Salem: April 23, 2012

They put me in a single cell with Yamen. Before we were arrested, I'd quarrelled with him because he sent love letters to my sister. In the cell they left me handcuffed and removed his cuffs, and when they brought us one boiled potato in the evening, Yamen peeled it and wanted to feed me the whole thing but I refused.

"Half for you and half for me," I said. These were the first words I'd spoken to him since the argument.

Once we'd finished the meal, which only took a few seconds, I confronted him with the question I'd wanted to ask him for a while: "Would you be happy if I wrote love letters to your sister?"

He smiled, showing the extra tooth that grew above his milk tooth.

"If only you would," he said. "You're a kind, intelligent guy, and my sister could never love a better person than you."

His response took me by surprise. I was going to begin a discussion about honor, love and shame with him, but the sound of the key in the cell door put a stop to any further talk. Two soldiers handcuffed Yamen again, and one of them shouted, "Fuck your mothers, sons of whores," and they began punching us as they led us out into a narrow corridor, then kicked us into a room where a man dressed in a white shirt sat stroking his moustache and looking at us like a cat about to pounce.

Our schoolbags were lying in front of him on the metal table. The interrogator opened Yamen's notebook and read: "'*I love you more than myself.*'" After a brief silence he asked, looking at Yamen, "Who's this whore you love? Is she the one who invited you to join the demonstration?"

When Yamen didn't reply, one of the soldiers began beating him ferociously: "The colonel's asking you a question. Answer, you animal."

"I write these things as if I'm writing poetry. I'm not addressing any girl in particular."

"Who invited you to take part in the demonstration?"

"I didn't take part in the demonstration."

The interrogator turned over the pages of the notebook and continued to read the letters: "'*When I kiss you, it will be the first kiss of love, and the world will turn into a paradise.*' Don't you like life? The world will turn into a paradise? And what do you mean by the first kiss? Are you planning to take part in subversive acts?"

"No never, I swear. The first kiss is the kiss I'll give the girl who I'll fall in love with one day."

"Are you going to keep lying? You're trying to make us look stupid, you bastard. I'll teach you what the first kiss is." Then he turned to address the soldier: "Abu'l-Layl, let him kiss your boot."

"Bend down and kiss this boot, animal."

Yamen didn't bend down. They beat him savagely. Blood poured from his nose and ears, but he didn't kiss the boot. They took us back to the cell without asking me a single question. Yamen was stony-faced, but when I patted his shoulder and gently embraced him, the tears he had been holding back began to run down his cheeks.

About an hour later, a different soldier opened the door.

"Which of you is the hero who doesn't obey orders?" he asked. Neither of us answered. He grabbed hold of our heads and banged them together. "You'll kiss everybody's boots, bastards."

When we arrived back in the room, they clubbed us repeatedly and bent Yamen backwards in the torture device called "the German chair" till I thought his spine would snap. His scream seemed to fill the whole world. Next they bent him forward so his mouth was against a soldier's boot.

"Kiss it, son of a bitch. Before we stuff this club up your ass. That'll teach you to take part in demonstrations."

When Yamen kissed the boot, the interrogator laughed.

"This is your first kiss," he said, "which you'll never forget."

I felt we were defeated. I didn't suffer the same torture as Yamen, perhaps because I responded to the command to kiss the boot before the blood came out of my ear and before my back was twisted in the German chair.

"Now who was it that invited the two of you to the demonstration?"

"We were going home from school," replied Yamen, "and we weren't in the demonstration."

"If you don't tell us, we'll kill you here."

"I swear to God," I said, "I passed the demonstration by chance when I was going home."

While we were being beaten again, the interrogator said to the soldiers, "They want freedom. Give them freedom till they're sick of it."

We returned to the cell broken, looking at each other apologetically, or as if we were embracing each other with our eyes.

8

Yamen: May 27, 2012

They released us after friends of Salem's father intervened on our behalf. Generous and affectionate, Salem's father was quick to invite me to attend the private lessons he had arranged for his son. He looked at me directly and said, "I don't want this year to be wasted, and I hope you and Salem will make up the lessons you missed. You have to pass ninth grade."

Salem came and took me with him to his house, along with books on mathematics, physics and English. After we'd been sitting together for a while, waiting for the first teacher, the phone rang. Salem picked it up.

"Hallo, yes, it's me. Coming." Heading for the door, he said, "Back in a few minutes. I'm going to pick up some vegetables and fruit my father bought and left in the shop."

When Salem had been gone for a while, Taima came in carrying a bag. She put it down and walked towards me. I remembered how they repeatedly ordered me to kiss their boots. I seemed incapable of protecting my fingers, my lips and my dreams. I felt as if my soul was crushed.

9

Taima: May 29, 2012

Yes, the miracle happened, and we were alone in the house, and I moved close to Yamen who'd come out of prison. I wanted to congratulate him and say a thousand sweet words to him, but all the words dried up as he sobbed and said things I didn't understand at the time. I found out, after my brother told us in detail what he and Yamen had been subjected to, why he was sobbing as if his soul was breaking in pieces. This time Yamen wrote me a longer letter than usual:

Don't be angry with me. I shall never love anyone like I love you. But they wrecked the first kiss I was saving for you and forced me to drop it on their boots.

I won't be angry with him. I'm waiting for the miracle to happen again so I can put my arms around him and give him the first kiss even if he's crying.

This was originally written in Damascus in 2012. It was lost and rewritten in Kingston, Ontario, in 2023.

The Ring

I couldn't suppress my anger.

"Are you defending him?" I shouted in my mother's face. "How can you let me sleep with a monster? I swear monsters are nicer than him."

My mother looked back at me with a reproachful expression, then said in a steady, calm voice, "I'll ignore the fact that you're screaming at your mother. I'm not defending him. I'm defending you and your children. Lamia, listen to me. Who's going to feed your kids? Who's even going to buy socks for them in these dark days?"

She was trying to make me change my mind, taking advantage of my attachment to my three children, but I was determined.

"You want me to live with a man I can't bear for the sake of food — and socks! Isn't that prostitution?"

My mother lost her temper, one of her tactics when she wanted to exercise her authority.

"What are you saying? Have you finally lost any sense of shame?"

"What am I saying? Listen to me. Being a whore is better than living like this. A whore knows men with different temperaments and ideas, and she isn't forced to spend all her time with someone she can't stand and—"

My mother interrupted me, her lips quivering as they usually did when she was really angry.

"How can you say that? Is this how I raised you? Comparing yourself to a whore? The man is your husband, and we didn't force you to marry him."

"That marriage was a curse. You pushed me into it after the death of my first husband. You all began giving me orders: 'You're a widow, you shouldn't wear bright colors, you shouldn't laugh, you shouldn't behave like normal people.' You were intent on watching my every move and you, my mother, actually disapproved of me and my children. When I tried to look for a job it was you who stopped me. 'Widows fall into the devil's clutches,' you said. 'You're a beautiful young woman, and your bosses will take advantage of you.' Do you remember?"

"You're exaggerating. We were giving you advice, looking out for you."

"You keep repeating 'we were looking out for you' so you can impose all the restrictions you want on me. I know better than you, better than anybody, what's good for me. And it's not good for me to live with a beast like him. I'm not an animal to be bought and kept like a slave in exchange for my food." I stood up. "In any case, I'm leaving," I said. "This no longer feels like a family home or a refuge to me."

I went to wake my children who were asleep in what used to be their uncle's room before he emigrated.

My mother blocked my path.

"Where are you going to go at night, you crazy woman? Don't wake your children up." Then she closed the door and leaned her back against it, repeating what she had said to me so many times, "You're a disaster. You're mad and you're heartless. And you don't care if you give me a stroke." She burst into tears. "Isn't Baha' enough for me to deal with?"

Baha' is my younger brother, who suffers from catalepsy.

Without a word I took her hand and led her over to the sofa. We sat there, both of us silently weeping, until my mother broke the silence.

"Give me a hanky," she said. I handed her a tissue and took one for myself and dabbed at my eyes and nose like her. The storm of anger and weeping subsided. My mother got up and brought me a pair of pajamas. I hugged her and realized I had left everything behind in the home I shared with my husband, including my pajamas. I lay down on her bed next to her, and we fell asleep, thinking about our ugly past and fearing an even more horrible future.

*

The following day, my mother took plastic bags out of the fridge. Without a word I took them from her and began chopping eggplants and tomatoes while she sliced onions, ready to make the moussaka. As we prepared the food, the children played in the courtyard beside the fountain. We put the pot on the stove, and I began washing the dishes piled up in the sink. I was thinking of the car accident that took my father's life. He was run over by a reckless driver from the Political Intelligence Branch.

“What happened, Lamia?” my mother asked me, reverting to the calm voice she used to hide her domineering tone.

*

I was going over what happened to myself as I cleaned the dishes and pots after lunch. I agreed to marry Zaidan a year after the death of my first husband and two years after my father’s death and a lot of angry exchanges between me and my mother, which always made me feel I was just a burden. I accepted Zaidan, a simple worker in Souq al-Hal vegetable market, and in the first few months of our marriage I learned he was an informer working with the Political Intelligence Branch. This was a big shock to me as I’d always considered such work low and despicable. The informer lives by eavesdropping on people’s thoughts and preparing reports on what people say about the regime. These reports result in torture and even death if there’s an urgent investigation that relies on the use of violence. On top of that, my father lost his life under the wheels of their car, and my brother Wassim received excessively harsh treatment at their hands. They arrested him when he talked after our father’s death about the recklessness and negligence of the intelligence services. When he was released, I saw with my own eyes the sorrow they had planted in his heart. He was no longer the lively young man he used to be and was silent and serious most of the time.

Before he left for Greece he said to me, “Once I found out what was going on in this country, I knew I was going to emigrate whatever the cost. We live among monsters, Lamia, and we’re liable to be abused at any time.”

I remembered my brother's words whenever Zaidan was trying to approach me and I would turn away from him, saying I had a headache or was in a bad mood because of my period. Once he asked me, "How many times a month do you get your period?" I told him nothing was regular in my life. It was all muddle and chaos.

When demonstrations swept the country, Zaidan volunteered in a militia in the People's Committees. He became the leader of a local group and used to talk to me confidently about his meeting with the head of the intelligence branch and other people whose names aroused fear in people's hearts.

When we spoke via Messenger, my brother Wassim said to me: "Don't be angry with me for saying this, but Zaidan is an insignificant player in this hellish machine the regime uses against us."

I certainly wasn't angry with Wassim, and I told him how Zaidan's walk had changed and how even the way he held himself was different after he joined the militia. He strutted about like a peacock in his military uniform with the red ribbon fixed to his left shoulder to identify the type of militia he worked for. He even boasted that he opened fire on a group of people in front of the neighborhood's communal oven, and they ran away like rats.

"Wouldn't you run away if you were being shot at and you were unarmed?" I asked him.

"A fighter doesn't run away," he said, puffing out his chest. "I confront the horrors head-on."

I remembered Zaidan before he carried a gun. He was afraid of his own shadow, thought everybody was his enemy and didn't feel safe going out at night.

*

Zaidan invited me and the children to have dinner at a luxurious restaurant where there was a special place for children to play.

"It's been a long time since we drank a cold beer outside the house," he said.

He wore an expensive new suit, and as we were getting ready to go out to dinner, he talked about buying a house in an upmarket neighborhood.

"Where will you get the money?" I asked.

He said he was working day and night.

Killing and robbing day and night, I said to myself.

I decided to put the washing in the machine before we went out. I searched through the pockets of the children's jackets and trousers, and found a pencil sharpener, a coin and, as usual, some tissues. I hated the way tissues disintegrated into little bits all over the washed clothes. In Zaidan's trouser pocket I saw a gold wedding ring. There were traces of blood on the pocket and even on the ring itself.

"Zaidan," I cried. "Who does this wedding ring belong to?"

Zaidan gave a coarse laugh. "Don't worry," he answered. "I'm not going to marry another woman."

"Where did you get this ring?" I asked, deadly serious.

"Off the finger of a dead rat."

"Did you kill the man and take his ring with traces of blood on it?"

"He was dead. The blood was from his swollen finger."

"Did you cut off his finger?"

"The dead don't need fingers or rings."

I couldn't bear to continue the discussion. Unable to control myself any longer, I blurted out, "The beer you're offering me tastes like the piss of the men you've killed. I don't want it. I don't want your dirty money."

"Have you gone crazy? What I'm doing is for you and your children. In war, this is the safest way to get what you need to live. In war, it's forbidden to die from your enemies' bullets or from starvation."

"And everything in our life becomes contaminated with people's blood? I don't want to be dragged any further into life with a criminal."

"What are you saying, bitch? This is war. If I don't kill my enemy, he will kill me. In war the spoils go to the victors. Do you understand or are you stupid as usual?"

I took the children's hands, preparing to leave. "And you justify your crimes as if they were inevitable," I said.

"How are we going to guarantee the medicine for your sick brother? How will we feed your old mother?"

"Do you want to purge your sins with a pill and a morsel of bread? We don't want them. Divorce me. Divorce me immediately."

I was out in the street when I heard him screaming like someone deranged: "Is this how you reward charity? What have I done, Lamia, you bitch? Come back! Come back here! If you don't come back, I'll blow you up, you and your children, and kill your brother, and you'll be food for stray dogs."

I took a taxi with the children to my mother's house. My neighbor Su'ad told me that when I left, he went down into the street and started swearing at me, hitting himself round the head and shouting, "How am I going to make that bitch understand? How am I going to make her understand?"

*

When my mother heard what had happened, she said quietly, "What are you going to do now?"

"I'm going to divorce the bastard."

Trying to trap me into thinking of the hard days ahead, she asked, "How will you feed your children . . . and how . . ."

She didn't finish the question but merely shook her head sorrowfully, as if to say, "There's no hope for you."

Damascus, 2012.

Beans, Beans, Beans

I

Forty years ago, the school principal told us we could attend the prize-giving ceremony without wearing our school uniform if we liked, and we could invite our parents to watch the prizes being distributed. I didn't like wearing the school uniform because the secondhand jacket my mother bought was too big for me. The sleeves covered my fingers, and she couldn't shorten them, but she managed to shorten the trousers so they fit me.

"I'm not going to school in this jacket. It's . . ." I told her.

Before I'd finished the sentence, she understood what I wanted and sorted things out as she always did. She turned the frayed shirt collar so the worn part where it rubbed against my neck was no longer visible, and she cut and hemmed the sleeves of the shirt so it became a summer shirt. She took me to the village cobbler, who mended my shoes and polished them till they shone.

"Look, they're just like new," she said smiling at me.

We both knew this wasn't true, as the polish couldn't cover up the worn patches on the sides of my shoes, but what she had done made me more confident about my clothes.

2

Neither my mother nor my father, who was always away, was there to be proud of me while the prizes were given out to the top students. Neither of them heard the praise I received on the stage. I was one of the very few students without parents in the audience. The principal said he was proud to have me as a pupil in his school, and the class teacher said he hadn't known a pupil as alert and intelligent and hardworking as me in all his 25 years in education, which embarrassed me but also made me feel very happy. I was eager to find out what was in the package the school principal had presented to me and desperately hoped it was a pair of white, high-end trainers, but I opened it and saw five books from the Successful People series, with the following titles: *al-Mutanabbi, Poet of the Arabs*; *Shakespeare, Poet of Mankind*; *Madame Curie Who Discovered Radium*; *Edison Who Lit Up the World*; *Leonardo da Vinci, the Immortal Painter*. Rather than thinking how I could be added to this series, I was thinking how to acquire a pair of white, solid, comfortable trainers.

On the way home I felt sharp pangs of hunger. My mother would reward me when I told her how I had been the center of attention. Every day she cooked us beans with olive oil and garlic. I would ask her to fry an egg for me — in fact, two eggs. Like all the other women in our village, my mother collected eggs to sell to the street vendor in exchange for the goods he carried on his donkey around the unpaved roads of the villages where there were no shops.

3

I entered the house and smelled beans. My mother had cooked green beans every day since the bean season began. I handed her my prize, smiling. Although she was illiterate, she took it and looked at it and then hugged me. She asked me to tell her what was written on it. I read out the names of the subjects and my marks in each subject.

"Is that good?" she asked, so I told her what the principal and the class teacher had said.

"I wished you or my father were in the audience," I added, "to hear for yourselves what Mr. Mansour and the principal said."

Her eyes filled with tears. She said without looking at me, as if she was talking to the air, "The sea has taken your father away. Who knows where he is. And I always have so much work on the land and in the house. The leaves of the tobacco seedlings have turned yellow, and I haven't had time to pick them yet."

I told her I wanted to eat eggs.

"I'll show you what I bought with the eggs," she said. "I gave them all to the street vendor."

I took my chance when a neighbor dropped in and left her talking to my mother and headed for my Aunt Souad's house. I didn't want to eat beans and hoped she had cooked something different. When I entered, my aunt was pouring beans cooked with oil and garlic into a large aluminum dish. She invited me to have lunch with her, and I said I'd just come to say hallo.

On the way to my uncle's house, I met the children of all four of my uncles. The same invitation was repeated in all the uncles' houses and all the pots contained the same thing: beans with oil and garlic. Two of my uncles' wives used the same expression, smiling as they said: "Come right in! You'll eat your fingers after the beans I've cooked."

As I went off to my Aunt Salma's house to see what she had on the stove, I wondered who invented the phrase "you'll eat your fingers after this." Pleasure makes you so greedy that you can't distinguish between your fingers and the food and you devour your fingers. I don't think anyone would eat his fingers with these beans and garlic.

Like the rest of my relatives, my aunt had cooked beans, so I decided to visit my cousin Layla, who'd only been married for a week. Why hadn't I thought of her to start with? The food was bound to be different during the honeymoon. On the way to my cousin's house, I heard Salwa, the mayor's daughter, saying, "Beans, beans, beans. I can't stand myself anymore because I've eaten so many beans. Beans, every day." And I heard her father, the mayor, singing the praises of beans just like my mother.

I was disappointed: Layla had cooked beans with garlic and oil like other women whose honeymoons ended long ago.

On my way home, as I passed in front of Abdu's house, I heard his wife saying, "We've eaten nothing but beans since the start of the bean harvest."

I arrived home. "I'm hungry," I said to my mother.

"Where have you been?" she asked.

"I was looking for something to eat that wasn't beans, but beans have invaded every home."

"Hunger is the best cook, as they say," smiled my mother. "When we're hungry, any food tastes delicious. Your cousins came and devoured all the beans I'd cooked. I'll pick some more and cook them for you right now."

"Don't we have any eggs?"

"I told you the peddler took all the eggs we had from our hens. In fact, we still owe him six eggs. You've reminded me."

My mother disappeared into her room and returned at once. Looking at me as if urging me to smile, she said, "Look. I asked the peddler to bring you these," and she held out a pair of white trainers.

"Come on! Try them." They were comfortable. I picked a few beans from the land in front of our house, and my mother cooked them for me. The next day she made sure to reward me with a fried egg, which she thought of as a prize for my performance at school.

4

Before we were forced to leave our home, my granddaughter used to say to her mother, "Why does my grandfather bring us 30 eggs every time he visits? Eggs, eggs, eggs! Does he want me to turn into a chicken?"

In the refugee camp, I would look at the members of my family, all of them starving, and remember the long bean season when we used to say, "Beans, beans, beans. Beans every day. When will the season end?"

And now in the tent it was, "Nothing, nothing, nothing. When will the season of nothing end?"

Damascus, 2012.

The Document

I

Hamdo, the old pickpocket, got off the bus and went to meet his fellow pickpocket and lifelong friend Raji. For half a century they had exchanged experiences and compared skills in the use of fingers and sharp blades to gain speedy access to the contents of people's pockets.

"I was on the bus from Damascus to al-Tall," said Hamdo as they drank tea together. "There was a man in his fifties who looked like the singer Farid al-Atrash, with a waxed moustache like al-Zir Salem's."

"But Farid al-Atrash doesn't have a moustache," remarked Raji with a laugh.

"The man looked like Farid al-Atrash if Farid al-Atrash had a moustache. The point is he had a treasure in the left inside pocket of his jacket, which he kept looking at throughout the journey."

"So why didn't you check out this treasure for yourself while you were on the bus?" asked Raji, exhaling smoke from his cigarette.

Hamdo cursed old age that made his fingers shaky and less agile, and Raji laughed again.

2

Maryam Salman welcomed her husband Abdullah back from Damascus.

"Tell me what happened," she said. "I can't wait to hear!"

Abdullah smiled and took a sheet of paper from the left inside pocket of his jacket as if it were a butterfly's fragile wings. He held it up in her face like a victory sign and took her in his arms.

"I met him," he said. "And we're going to visit him. Our son, Yusuf."

Her eyes filled with tears of joy. "You have to tell me the whole story from beginning to end after we've had dinner," she said wiping away her tears.

Maryam had decided to make yabraq, stuffed vine leaves, Abdullah's favourite dish, and she was happy when he said as he ate with relish, "You're the best cook in the world and the most beautiful woman."

After dinner Maryam sat down opposite him.

"Now tell me," she said.

Abdullah described his trip at length as Maryam drank in his words with her eyes, ears and, indeed, her whole being. He told her about the huge wooden door of the villa, which resembled the door of a fortress, and the guards with guns and the gleaming floor and his embarrassment at his dirty shoes and the marks they left on the doormat and how alien they appeared beside everything else in the villa. He told her about the woman who received him, whom he thought must be the wife of the big man, but he neglected to mention her rosy heels and the roundness of her thighs, which was revealed when she crossed her legs. He talked about the cigarette she was smoking, the two fine gold bands on it and the lipstick-stained filter and the big man's arrival in the room and his warm welcome.

"He welcomed me as if he'd known me for a thousand years and said he wished he could live contentedly in the village and pick grapes and figs with his own hands. As you'll notice, Maryam, these bastards like to reap and not to sow. The big man told me Safi had delivered the agreed amount to him. Imagine, Maryam, they call the bribe they demanded from us 'the agreed amount.' It's the price of the land Safi bought from me, land that has no equal in the village of al-Tall. Do you remember when we planted it with lettuce and tomatoes and cucumber, and there was enough for the whole village? There wasn't a single person in al-Tall who didn't eat the good things it produced. It's extremely fertile land, where the crops are happy and give in abundance, not to mention the view it commands and the sweetness of its air. That bastard Safi exploited our need to know what was happening to our son."

"Don't be angry, Abdullah. We're all going to die one day, and we can't take anything with us to the grave. And Yusuf, our son, we want to know whether he's alive or . . ."

"Trust in God, Maryam. My heart tells me he's alive, but that bastard Safi doesn't even deserve to set foot on this land, and yet he's the only one in our village who can afford to buy it."

"Just tell me what happened. What did the big man say?"

"I asked him how Yusuf was and when he would be released. He cleared his throat and said, 'I don't want to lie to you. Nobody knows when Yusuf, or any of the political prisoners, will be released except the Lord above and Mr. President.' Then he said, 'We must hope for the best.'" (Abdullah did not tell her that the big man said these prisoners have committed an unforgiveable crime.)

"But our son wasn't political," said Maryam tearfully. "He went to Hama to bring his sister and her children home while the city was under siege, as any brother in the world would do."

"We're doomed, Maryam. Those people don't have hearts."

"So what happened next?"

"The man looked at his watch and said he was late for his shift, told me about all his great responsibilities and promised me he'd contact the governor of Tadmur prison and I'd be able to visit my son. Then he asked Su'ad for a piece of paper. The maid, the woman I'd thought was his wife, stood up and brought him a sheet of plain paper and a pen with a gold nib, and the man wrote something on the paper."

Abdullah took the piece of paper from his jacket pocket again and read aloud to Maryam: "'*We hereby authorize you to enable the bearer of this document to visit his son Yusuf Abdullah al-Mas'ud and to ensure the safety of him and his son.*' Then there's a signature."

Jabbing his finger at the signature, Abdullah held the paper out to Maryam.

"This is the signature, Maryam. Look at it." Then he counted the words. "Twenty-eight words and a signature. This is the price of the land."

"The price of the land is the signature, Abdullah. Anyone can write those words."

"You're right, you're absolutely right. The point is the land's now in the hands of that lowlife Safi, and I no longer have the right to sit in the shade of the apricot tree in its western corner. But as you said, we don't take anything with us to our graves and the joy we'll feel when we see Yusuf is worth all the riches in the world. Money is only paper after all, and this piece of paper is more important than any money because we will see Yusuf and make sure he's okay."

They talked for a long while and decided to go and see Yusuf the next morning. Maryam couldn't sleep. She remembered Yusuf's laugh and the way he hugged her when she packed dried figs for him to take to Damascus the year he moved to study at the university there. She remembered his love of apples, and of his pistachio-green shirt.

"I love the color of this shirt," he'd said. It wasn't exactly green, but white with a hint of green. She decided to buy him a shirt of the same color, and winter pajamas and summer pajamas and underwear and a towel. She wished she could pack the whole world into a bag, and all the freedom in the world, and take it for him to enjoy in the desert prison of Tadmur.

3

In the city of Homs, Maryam found things she wanted to buy for Yusuf, and the goods on display in the shop windows made her think of more things. As she carried the plastic bags and packages to the car, Abdullah Mas'ud paid and smiled magnanimously.

4

On the way to Tadmur prison in the desert, Abdullah was imagining the big man contacting the prison governor: "Yusuf Abdullah al-Mas'ud. Yes. That's the prisoner's name. His father, Abdullah al-Mas'ud, and his mother, Maryam, will visit him. Please see that they are looked after."

The phones were ringing in Abdullah's head and he heard the conversation between the big man and the prison governor again and again. In the back seat Maryam was remembering Yusuf's childhood, which remained vivid in her mind even though Yusuf had left her over a quarter of a century before.

5

When they reached the point where cars were obliged to halt, Abdullah al-Mas'ud and Maryam got out of the yellow taxi. Abdullah walked confidently towards the gate, smiling because he had the document safely in the inside pocket of his jacket. One of the military policemen guarding the gate ordered Abdullah and Maryam to stop, but Abdullah reached into his pocket and took out the document, opened it and stepped towards the policeman.

"Are you an idiot?" shouted the policeman angrily. "Don't you know what stop means?"

The insult took Abdullah by surprise, so he took another step forward, protected by the vital signature on the document. The policeman pushed him back, and he collided with Maryam, who fell to the ground, her purchases scattering around her. Abdullah helped her to her feet, and they picked the things up and he brushed off the dust that was clinging to her clothes.

I'll tell the prison governor this won't do. He'll reprimand the stupid policeman and apologize to me and Maryam because this fool doesn't know the value of the signature or how much it cost. It would be beneath me to spit in the bastard's face. All the same, I have to be nice to him as he still has Yusuf's fate in his hands.

Abdullah stood still, his eyes fixed on the policeman's black moustache and red beret. The policeman approached him angrily, and Abdullah held out the document to him. He snatched it from Abdullah and tore it into pieces and threw them in the air; some of them blew around and others fell to the ground.

6

In the village of al-Tall, Safi was strolling about the land he had bought so cheaply from Abdullah al-Mas'ud, like a fisherman who has landed a precious catch.

The blood rushed to Abdullah's head, and he realized he had been humiliated in the same way that the land he loved had been humiliated. He remembered the torn bits of the document blowing around in the air, and it occurred to him that Safi was just doing the big man's dirty work and that all big men were crooks. He walked onto the land, and Safi thought he had come to pick up the axe he'd left by the apricot tree. When Safi approached him, he couldn't stop himself raising the axe and bringing it down on Safi's head. He returned the axe to its place and sat where he usually sat under the apricot tree in the west corner. It was as if he didn't see the uproar around him, didn't see them dragging Safi's body away, and when the police came to arrest him, he welcomed them. Maryam saw them putting cuffs on his wrists, and he didn't look at anyone, even Maryam, although she was uttering shrill cries of celebration mixed with lamentation and tears were pouring down her cheeks.

Saydnaya prison, 1988.

My Grandmother Fatima's Cough

1

When we returned to our house in Yarmouk camp in the summer of 2020, there was no furniture left. Weeping, my mother named every piece of furniture and reminded us how she had sold her earrings to buy the sofa she'd fallen in love with. My father enumerated the stolen items as he called my uncle, who was a refugee in Jordan:

"They've stolen everything, even the door and windows. They pulled the electric wiring out of the wall, man, stole the water tank and the taps. Everything, everything, my brother."

To me the house looked naked, desecrated, violated. My grandmother Fatima told me how her family house had been desecrated in Tantura in Palestine in 1948.

"The house was unable to defend us," she said. "But it still weeps for us."

When I laughed she said reproachfully: "Don't laugh. Houses have hearts that yearn and weep."

2

My grandmother Fatima died in my arms on the prayer rug in the Omari Mosque in the town of Qudsaya. She died wearing the sandy dress she loved. She was the one who named it "the sandy dress" because it was the color of sand. It was one of the few things she took with her when we were displaced from Yarmouk camp. A few hours before she died, she smiled and repeated the phrase she often used to praise me.

"You're the firstborn of the firstborn," she said, implying that this fact granted me superior status among her grandchildren.

My grandmother's smile was so sweet you felt as if her whole face, and even her dress, were smiling. I told her I hadn't chosen to be the firstborn and couldn't claim any credit for it. She frowned. Pointing to a pot of roses that one of the women displaced from Yarmouk had brought with her and placed at the door of the mosque, she said, "And did that rose choose to be beautiful?" She was silent for a while, before adding with her irresistible smile, "Did the gazelles of Rantis choose to have beautiful eyes?" She winked so I would understand she meant to compliment my eyes, which she had frequently compared to the eyes of the gazelles of Rantis in Palestine. Then she was overcome by a coughing fit, and I rushed to give her some tissues. The box of tissues was one of the few things I brought with me when I left the camp because I was haunted by my grandmother's needs.

3

We left the camp walking in a crowd of people, my aunt muttering, "This is the fifth time I've been displaced."

My brother Hakim, who was seven years old, brought his face as close to mine as he could and said, "What about you? How many times have you been displaced, Maryam?"

I looked at him. "I'm like you," I said, trying my best to hide the sadness that overwhelmed me. "This is the first time I've had to leave the house where I was born."

"How many times does a person have to be displaced in their life?" asked Hakim.

"Why are you asking?"

"So I know how many more times I have left," he replied gravely.

My grandmother hugged him in the middle of the crowded road and said, "Only God knows."

Like my father who was leading us, Hakim looked lost. He ran to keep up with us but soon grew tired and begged us to walk more slowly.

My aunt was muttering things we didn't understand, and didn't need to understand, since she wasn't addressing any of us. Wiping her tears on the sleeve of her brown overcoat, she talked to the air, which seemed heavy with our sorrows.

4

In the camp I used to spend part of the day making sure my grandmother's room was clean and noticing what she needed, tissues in particular. My grandmother was obsessed with cleanliness, but she suffered from a severe chronic cough. In the last year, before we left the camp and took refuge in the Omari Mosque, I'd grown accustomed to hearing her say after every bout of coughing, "This time I'm going to die. I'm really going to die."

I was also used to seeing my mother's tears whenever my grandmother hurled her prophesies of death into the room. She would repeatedly plead with my grandmother not to mention the word *death*, which came without any of the usual invocations to ward off evil.

"Mother, surely you're used to her constant talk of death by now?" I asked.

"We are surrounded by death on all sides," replied my mother, her eyes filling with tears again. "It restricts our past and our present. Death is ugly, and I don't like people mentioning it in front of me."

My grandmother smiled and covered her mouth with her hand.

"Your mother's very sensitive," she whispered to me, "but she's talking nonsense."

"The doctors are puzzled by your grandmother's cough, and so are we," remarked my father one day.

Doctor Ahmad, famous for his medical expertise, said, "God knows what kind of allergy causes this cough."

The truth is that secretly, so as not to upset Doctor Ahmad, my father took my grandmother to see other doctors, but they were equally baffled by the bouts of coughing. My grandmother tells me that she held her breath and suppressed her cough when she was in hiding, during the Tantura massacre in Palestine.

"I was young," she said. "I stopped myself coughing as I ran along beside my mother towards the village of Fureidis at the foot of Mount Carmel. I saw how they put men in barrels, men I knew." She sighed and looked towards the window as if her eyes were drilling through the glass and the weight of accumulated time. "That day the hot weather had begun, and the wheat was ready for harvesting. No more than a few weeks after the founding of Israel, the newborn Israeli army shelled our village and attacked it with firearms. People called these soldiers the 'Alexandroni Brigade.' They forced the men to climb into the barrels and opened fire on them. I heard the voices of the trapped men and saw blood flowing from the holes left by the bullets in the bodies in the barrels that summer. They say they forced our people to dig trenches and then buried them there. My son, Zahdi, says they levelled the ground over the dead men and turned it into a parking lot."

My mother cries. My mother cries if a branch snaps in the wind. My grandmother's tales are full of stories of death, displacement, poverty and the ingenious ways people find to carry on living when times are hard.

"Your mother's crying as if the past is with us in this living room," said my grandmother smiling. "We have to think of our today and our tomorrow. What's the point of crying?"

"Your grandmother is strong," said my mother. "She can make fun of everything, even death."

My grandmother tried all kinds of cough medicine and all the herbs advised by herbalists. We boiled thyme and ginger for her, and when my Aunt Fathiyya was displaced from Nahr al-Bared camp near Tripoli in Lebanon and came to live with us, she recommended another new treatment, rubbing my grandmother's chest with black seed oil and from time to time feeding her a teaspoon of the oil. My grandmother used to say she'd rather cough than take this medicine, but when my aunt gave me a spoonful it didn't taste as horrible as my grandmother made it out to be. Maybe she was joking or being melodramatic.

Aunt Fathiyya was displaced from Nahr al-Bared camp in 2007 during the war between the Lebanese army and Fatah al-Islam, and my father welcomed her into our home in Yarmouk camp. She talks about the horrors in Nahr al-Bared, where she lost her only son during the bombing of the camp. My mother started to cry again. My aunt said her tears have dried and she has wept for all the widows and bereaved mothers in the world. She laughed and then burst into floods of tears again. Her husband died during the Israeli invasion of Lebanon in 1982. He was selling grilled corn on the cob in the street when a stray bullet ended his life. My aunt insists it wasn't a stray bullet: "We Palestinians don't die from stray bullets. We die from intended bullets."

My mother loved Aunt Fathiyya, and my grandmother agreed to let her share her bedroom. This room was small with a single bed and no room for another bed unless we took the table out. Aunt Fathiyya said she would sleep in the living room on the metal sofa, but my grandmother insisted she sleep in her room and replaced the big table with a small table. My father bought a secondhand sofa that opened out to make a bed, and the room became a bedroom for my grandmother and aunt. I continued to be a regular visitor there, perhaps because I enjoyed my grandmother's obvious love for me.

5

On December 17, 2012, my father decided we should leave Yarmouk camp, and none of us objected.

"Death follows us wherever we go," declared my aunt. "It would have been better to die in Palestine."

"Now I'm going to die," repeated my grandmother.

My mother cried as usual while she packed everybody's suitcases and looked at the sofa she had bought with the money from the sale of her earrings. She had a tale to tell about every piece of furniture in our house. After the Russian MiGs bombed the heart of the camp and Abd al-Qadir al-Husseini Mosque, my father said, "The important thing is that we all survived. None of us died."

The crowd grew bigger as we went on. A man walking near me said, "In Palestine, American F16s bomb us, and here it's Russian MiGs. It is as if they're developing aircraft to test them on us."

We didn't know where we were going. My father was like a wounded bird. He had no idea where his feet were taking him. All the same, we followed him in a human stream, the like of which I had never witnessed before. We left the camp, and in the Maidan Gate neighborhood my father managed to charge his cell phone at a restaurant, where we ate ful beans and hummus. As soon as the battery regained some power, the phone rang. Abu Khalil, our bald neighbor who always wore a white shirt and thick glasses, was on the other end of the line.

"You can go to the Omari Mosque in Qudsaya," he told my father.

That was the first time I'd heard of this place. My grandmother didn't cough the whole way there, but as soon as we reached the mosque she started to cough violently, as if compensating for the time she had spent without speaking or coughing or even sighing.

6

During our stay in the Omari Mosque with more than a hundred displaced people from the camp, Abu Khalil talked about the killing of two hundred people in Abd al-Qadir al-Husseini Mosque.

"And here we are, taking refuge in a mosque again," said Abu Yasin. "How do we know it won't be bombed too?"

My mother, like all the women, took great care of the bundle she kept hidden inside her bra. It contained her wedding ring and some cash she was secretly saving.

In the mosque my grandmother felt her end was approaching, and she, too, had a bundle of precious things hidden inside her bra. Her coughing fits grew more severe, but her resolve had weakened considerably. Leaning on my shoulder as we went to the bathroom, she began to speak again.

"In Tantura," she said, "the soldiers put my father into one of those barrels. His smothered voice still haunts me. He was one of the dead men inside the barrels, but my ears picked up his death rattle, and that's when the cough started. Doctors don't know the cure for it. I'll recover the day I return to our home there in Tantura and then I'll get rid of it at once."

7

That evening my grandmother said, "Death seems closer than ever now. I don't want you to inherit this cough from me."

She took out her bundle and gently opened it, then began to bequeath its contents to me in front of all the people seeking refuge in the mosque. She held out a green bank note.

"This is a Palestinian pound that my father gave me to give to my Uncle Salim, but he died with my father on the day of the massacre."

Then she gave me a single gold earring.

"My husband gave me these earrings," she said laughing. "I lost the other one on our exodus from Beirut to Damascus."

Next she handed me an old key that she had kept polished and shiny.

"This is the key to our house in Tantura," she said. "This is the most important thing you're going to inherit." She laughed again. "You'll inherit the worry, generation after generation, until we return to Tantura and open our houses with these keys. You may not find the door," she added, "but you'll find a wall in a house where you can hang this key."

My grandmother made me promise to bathe her in the fountain set aside for women's ablutions in the mosque, and we agreed that I would arrange her hair nicely when she died and bury her in her sandy dress.

"I think it's suitable for meeting the Lord," she said smiling.

My grandmother confused me and I didn't know if she meant what she said or was just making fun of everything.

That evening she talked a lot about her journey from Palestine to Sidon, then to Tyre, Beirut and eventually Damascus. Her memory seemed as clear as a stream and flowed as gently. Many of the displaced people gathered around her and listened to her recount her history full of pain and witnessed the sweet way she spoke. They also witnessed her final coughing fit, which ended this time with her dying in my arms as I sat on a prayer rug in the Omari Mosque in Qudsaya in Damascus. Now I, like my mother and grandmother, carry a small bundle hidden in my bra, which contains the key to our house in Tantura, a single earring and a Palestinian pound.

Kingston, Ontario, February 2024.

Acknowledgments

It goes without saying that I owe my wife, Rufaida, and my two sons, Ghamr and Taim, immense gratitude, always.

I am deeply grateful to my cellmates, especially Yaser Makhlouf, Hussain Mohammed, Imadeddin Zabian, Ali Barazi, Jaffan al-Homsi, Musab al-Nabhan, Faiq Huwaija and Wael Sawah, who read the stories written in prison and encouraged me to write more.

Sergeant Yousef helped me to smuggle my stories from the prison. I'd like to thank him again from the bottom of my heart.

It is not easy to find the words to express my gratitude toward Catherine Cobham. She translates these stories through the eyes of Syria. Catherine was not only a translator but also a reader and editor, as well as an advisor. I can't find the words to do justice to her generosity.

My friends, writers Frances Itani and Lawrence Scanlon, deserve to be considered my two guardian angels. They always give me the sense that I'm not a stranger in my new homeland and the energy to continue writing. These words can never be enough to express my gratitude to them.

I am most grateful for the precious trust shown in me and my writing by Michael Holmes. Along with everyone at ECW Press, Michael made me feel that this establishment was not only my family in the field of writing and publishing but also close friends in my new homeland.

Many thanks to Victoria Cozza, Jennifer Gallinger, Jess Albert, Claire Pokorchak, Elham Ali and the rest of the staff at ECW Press, who are all so kind.

Special thanks to Kenna Barnes and Jennifer Foster for their professional readings.

And many thanks to my friend Asmaa Ali, who supplied a piece of art for the cover.

Jamal Saeed is a Syrian author, editor, visual artist, Arabic calligrapher, and translator. He worked in publishing and cofounded Friends of Art & Literature, which supports young Syrian creators. When secret intelligence threatened members, the organization dissolved. Jamal spent 12 years in a Syrian prison as a prisoner of conscience. Saeed landed in Canada with his family as a refugee in 2016. In 2020, he published *Yara's Spring*, a children's novel coauthored with Sharon McKay. His memoir, *My Road from Damascus*, was published to critical acclaim by ECW Press in 2022.

Entertainment. Writing. Culture.

ECW is a proudly independent, Canadian-owned book publisher. We know great writing can improve people's lives, and we're passionate about sharing original, exciting, and insightful writing across genres.

Thanks for reading along!

We want our books not just to sustain our imaginations, but to help construct a healthier, more just world, and so we've become a certified B Corporation, meaning we meet a high standard of social and environmental responsibility — and we're going to keep aiming higher. We believe books can drive change, but the way we make them can too.

Being a B Corp means that the act of publishing this book should be a force for good – for the planet, for our communities, and for the people that worked to make this book. For example, everyone who worked on this book was paid at least a living wage. You can learn more at the Ontario Living Wage Network.

This book is also available as a Global Certified Accessible™ (GCA) ebook. ECW Press's ebooks are screen reader friendly and are built to meet the needs of those who are unable to read standard print due to blindness, low vision, dyslexia, or a physical disability.

The interior of this book is printed on Sustana EnviroBook™, which is made from 100% recycled fibres and processed chlorine-free.

ECW's office is situated on land that was the traditional territory of many nations including the Wendat, the Anishnaabeg, Haudenosaunee, Chippewa, Métis, and current treaty holders the Mississaugas of the Credit. In the 1880s, the land was developed as part of a growing community around St. Matthew's Anglican and other churches. Starting in the 1950s, our neighbourhood was transformed by immigrants fleeing the Vietnam War and Chinese Canadians dispossessed by the building of Nathan Phillips Square and the subsequent rise in real estate value in other Chinatowns. We are grateful to those who cared for the land before us and are proud to be working amidst this mix of cultures.

ecwpress.com